A New
Dawn

JACK WEYLAND

Deseret Book

Salt Lake City, Utah

First printing February 1984
Second printing June 1984

Library of Congress Cataloging in Publication Data

Weyland, Jack, 1940—
    A new dawn.

    I. Title.
PS3573.E99N4   1984   813'.54   83-24049
ISBN 0-87747-994-1

CHAPTER ONE

It was Saturday night, and Lisa Salinger had a problem.

Actually three problems. The first was her graduate research project assigned by Dr. Owens, her adviser at Princeton University. She'd already spent three months on it and had gotten nowhere. It was no wonder—Einstein spent the last twenty years of his life searching for a solution to the same problem, and he never found the answer either.

Her second problem was that she wasn't going home for Christmas. Dr. Owens had asked her to stay in New Jersey over the holidays so they could get some research done.

To top it all off, her roommate Kimberly Brown was coming up the stairs with Hal. Lisa couldn't stand him.

She wrapped the old sheepskin coat tightly around her in case Hal came in. She'd picked up the knee-length coat the previous summer at a garage sale in her hometown of Fargo, North Dakota. She wore the coat over her flannel nightgown to keep warm against the damp winter nights.

She looked at the clock. It was eleven-thirty. She'd have to go to bed soon, or she'd be too tired to sing in church the next morning. She enjoyed singing in the choir of the First Methodist Church.

Hal and Kimberly were talking just outside the door. "Thanks again, Hal. The movie was a lot of fun. See you tomorrow for lunch, okay?"

"Wait, don't go in yet. It's still early. Let me come in for a few minutes. We could listen to records or watch TV." There was a pause, which meant he was kissing Kimberly. "Sometimes I get to feeling so lonely. Just for a while, okay?"

Kimberly sighed. "I'll ask, but you know what a bear she is."

The door opened. Lisa frantically began scribbling equations in hopes of discouraging Kimberly.

"I'm back," Kimberly called out. "Gee, you look busy."

"I am busy," Lisa said abruptly, breaking the point on her pencil for emphasis. She grabbed another pencil and continued.

Kimberly paused. "Hal wants to come in and play records for a while. He says he's lonely."

"If he's lonely, buy him a gerbil for Christmas," Lisa snapped.

"We'll keep the volume way down so you can study."

"I can't study with him around."

"Why not?"

"Because he's a jerk."

Kimberly paused. "Well, how about if you go to the storeroom for a while, like you do when I have a party."

Lisa turned to face Kimberly. "Why do I pay rent here? I spend all my time in the storeroom—your whole life is one party after another."

"You sound just like my mother. By the way, if she ever calls, don't tell her about the parties. She thinks I'm studying this semester."

"Just once I'd like to get some work done in my own apartment."

"Lisa, be reasonable. You've had four hours to study while we've been gone. Isn't that enough? C'mon, just for half an hour."

A minute later Lisa opened the door of the apartment on her way to the storeroom.

"Hi, Lisa," Hal said. "Busy on a term paper, huh?"

She gave him what she hoped was a withering stare. It didn't faze him.

"You work too hard. Me, I buy all my term papers. There's this company . . . I've got the catalog if you want to look at it sometime. It'd save you a lot of work." He flexed his arms. "Hey, how do you like my biceps now? Coming right along, huh? My roommate got me started. We go four times a week. You've probably noticed the difference in my arms and chest lately. Give me three months, and the girls are gonna go crazy." He flexed his muscles again. "How about that? Speaking as a woman, how is it to look at a Real Man?"

"I'll let you know if I ever see one." She turned and walked away.

On the way to the storeroom, she passed a pay phone in the hall. She decided to call home, using the telephone credit card she'd received in the mail a few weeks earlier.

As the phone rang, Lisa imagined the small apartment in Fargo where her mother and sister lived. They hadn't always been in an apartment. Up until she was in the seventh grade, they'd lived on a small farm, but after her parents' divorce, they'd moved into town.

Her mother answered.

"Hi, Mom."

"Lisa, is anything wrong?"

"Everything's fine—I just wanted to wish you a merry Christmas."

"The same to you. Oh, we got your package today. Thanks, but are you sure you can't come?"

"I'd better not. My research adviser wants me to stay and work."

"How's school going?"

"It's okay."

"Well, if you ever decide it's too much, you can always come home."

"I know, Mom."

"I wrote you a letter today. We've got big news back here. Karen's getting married."

Karen was her eighteen-year-old sister, three years younger than Lisa.

"She is? Who to?"

"A young man named David Passey. They met at work. It looks like it might be in May, but they keep moving it up."

"Karen's getting married?" Lisa said, trying not to sound threatened that her baby sister was getting married first.

"Well, I say she's too young, but you know how it is when a girl meets Mr. Wonderful."

"Can I talk to her now?"

"She's out on a date, but I'll tell her you called."

"Tell her I'm very happy for her."

"I will, dear."

There was a long pause. "Well, I guess I'd better hang up now. 'Bye, Mom."

As she started for the storeroom, she saw Mike Anderson coming down the hall. He was a graduate student from Utah, working toward a master's degree. She wrapped the sheepskin coat around her and hoped he'd just nod and pass by.

"Hi, Lisa," he said, stopping. "Kimberly having another party?"

"Not really—she and Hal are playing records, but I can't study with him around."

"I got a letter from Val today," he said, referring to his fiancée. "I told her you had some questions about BYU. She sent you a catalog."

Lisa shrugged her shoulders. "She didn't need to go to all that trouble. I was just curious about their physics program."

"Well, I've got the catalog, if you want to take it now."

She walked with him to his apartment. He let her in

and went to try to find the catalog. She said hello to his
roommate.

Once she'd been in Hal's apartment with Kimberly.
After seeing that, the most remarkable thing to her about
Mike's apartment was that there were no centerfold post-
ers on the wall, no pyramid of empty beer cans, and no
stolen road signs.

He gave her the catalog and showed her a new picture of Val.

A few minutes later she shuffled downstairs in her
old slippers to the storeroom and opened the door. The
room was full of suitcases, trunks, and junk left by gener-
ations of previous tenants—a pair of long wooden skis, a
lawnmower, three broken bicycles. It smelled of dust and
mildew, and it was cold. A dim lightbulb in the center of
the ceiling lit up the room just enough to emphasize its
ugliness.

Lisa unzipped the sleeping bag on the old cot and
crawled in. She wanted to sleep, but it was useless.

Her baby sister was getting married.

The next morning as she got ready for church, Lisa
paused to study her image in the bathroom mirror. More
than anything she looked efficient. Her short brown hair
was styled to reduce the time spent fussing over it. Her
wire-frame glasses made her look intellectual and a little
bored with life. She wore no makeup, and there was a
perpetual frown on her face.

I used to smile, she thought. *Where did it go?*

As a child she'd been happy enough. On the farm in
North Dakota, there were trees to climb and always a lit-
ter of kittens to play with. In the summer, the sweet smell
of alfalfa filled the air. A small pond across the road was
stocked with enough fish to make it worth the time spent
sitting on the bank watching a red plastic bobber in the
water. A girl Lisa's age lived on the farm next to them,

and she had a horse. Sometimes she let Lisa ride it.

Yes, she had smiled often enough when she was young.

But then one day in the seventh grade, her father announced he didn't love his wife anymore. He'd met someone else, someone younger.

The divorce proceedings became a war of accusations and legal maneuvers. The farm was sold, and her mother moved the family into a small apartment in Fargo and got a job in a hardware store.

After that, the three of them scrimped by. There was little money; kids at school made fun of Lisa because the clothes her mother bought for her at garage sales were made for short mature women and not for a seventh grader. They looked baggy and awful on her.

Sometimes being thirteen years old seemed like a prison sentence. A growth spurt suddenly turned her body into a war zone. Almost overnight she grew taller and her movements became awkward. Her face broke out. She became moody and spent days sulking in the bedroom shared unwillingly with Karen.

Just before school started the next year, her mother said, "If you want to go to college, you'll have to do it on your own, because I can't help you. Maybe if you study hard and get good grades from now on, you'll be able to get a scholarship."

Realizing the alternative to college might be spending life like her mother, sorting nuts and bolts into bins in a hardware store, Lisa focused her attention on school. Sometime in the process she discovered she was smart, especially in mathematics. Some boys seemed to resent how quickly she learned, but she didn't care.

She fell into the role of being the achiever, and her sister became lovable and sweet. Both were survival tactics.

Lisa looked critically at her reflection in the mirror. So what if Karen got married? It didn't matter. Lisa had a career to think about.

That Sunday before Christmas, Lisa enjoyed church because the choir sang four selections from Handel's *Messiah*. It was her favorite music. She'd read that when Handel wrote it, he stayed in his room for days in a surge of creative energy. What a thrill it'd be to create something that could stand the test of time.

When she returned from church, she found Kimberly and Hal having lunch. She opened the refrigerator, took out an apple, a carton of yogurt, and a pile of wheat sprouts.

"Hey, Lisa," Hal asked, "you got any games for your computer?"

"Oh, good grief," she mumbled. "Hal, this isn't an arcade."

She realized she was scowling again. She did that a lot around men. It was another of her defense mechanisms. Once at a roller skating rink when she was fifteen, she'd smiled at an older boy as he skated past her. A minute later he started skating with her. He was a good skater, and she was pleased he'd chosen her out of all the girls at the rink. They skated for a while, and then it was time to go. He offered to give her a ride home, and she accepted.

He drove out in the country and parked the car, then scooted over and tried to put his arm around her. She moved away.

And then he gave her a look she never forgot. It was as if she weren't really a person—as if she were only an obstacle to be overcome. She panicked and opened the door and jumped out.

He demanded to know what was the matter, saying that he hadn't even touched her.

She couldn't answer—she was too scared to make the words heard.

He accused her of leading him on.

She didn't understand how accepting an offer of a ride home could be misread to mean anything other than that she wanted a ride home.

He got out of the car and started walking toward her.

"What's wrong with you anyway? I'm not gonna hurt you." He was getting closer.

She turned and ran away. He swore at her, then got in his car and roared away, leaving her stranded. She had to walk home.

From then on, she adopted a perpetual frown because she believed that to smile around guys was inviting trouble.

"So, what do you use your computer for if you don't play games on it?" Hal said.

"It's a computer, Hal. I use it to compute," she said.

"And I suppose it'd be too much trouble to buy a couple of games for your friends to use on it once in a while?"

"Friends? You mean you, Hal?"

He laughed. "I know why you're so uptight all the time. You need a man in your life."

"That's the last thing I need."

To avoid being around Hal, she took her food to the storeroom, sat on the cot, and ate. Afterwards she decided to take a nap.

An hour later she woke up to the sound of gentle scratching. She looked down and saw a mouse finishing what she'd left in the yogurt container.

"Hello," she whispered.

The mouse froze.

"It's all right. You can eat it. I'm through."

The mouse stared at her, then cautiously moved toward the yogurt container.

"What's your name?" she asked gently.

He ran away and hid behind a suitcase.

"I know why you're afraid. You're two inches tall, and I'm sixty-six inches tall. So it'd be the same as if I came across a monster thirty-three times taller than me. Let's see . . . that'd be . . . about 180 feet high. I can understand your reluctance to come out while I'm here, but I mean no harm. I think I'll call you Maynard. Maynard Mouse. How does that sound?"

She could see him peeking from around a suitcase.
Kimberly opened the door. Maynard disappeared.
"Hal's gone now."
"Good."
"Were you talking to someone?"
"A mouse. We ate lunch together."
Kimberly laughed. "You've got to get out more. How
about meeting one of Hal's roommates?"
"Not if he's like Hal."
"It beats talking to mice," Kimberly said.
"It's the same thing," she answered.

Monday morning Lisa took her research notebook to
Dr. Owens's office for their weekly research meeting. Because it was Christmas vacation, the building was nearly
empty. Just before entering his office, she reached down
and pulled out of her book bag what looked like a
textbook. Actually it was a book cover glued onto a cigar
box. Inside the box was a small tape recorder. She used it
to tape lectures and research meetings. She did it secretly
because some professors wouldn't want what they said in
class to be recorded. She'd never told anyone about the
tape recorder.
Dr. Owens opened the door. He looked surprised to
see her.
"If it's not convenient, I'll come back later."
"No, no, come in."
She sat down.
"Well, what have you got this week?" he asked.
The phone rang. He answered it. ". . . What does she
want? . . . The house . . . What else? . . . How much per
month? . . . That's out of the question. What's she trying
to do, bankrupt me? I won't pay it . . . Well, you're the
lawyer, you work it out."
A minute later he hung up the phone. "Women," he
muttered.
The phone rang again.

"Hello," he said angrily. Then his voice softened. "Sorry, Sugar, I just got off the phone with my lawyer. My wife's trying to break me . . . She wants everything. Sugar Doll, I got our tickets . . . We'll be staying at a condo on Maui . . . It'll be great to be with you too . . . Look, I can't talk now, there's someone in my office . . . No, just a graduate student . . . Yes, it's a she . . ." He laughed. "Believe me, you have nothing to worry about . . . All right, see you tonight."

He hung up. None of it was news to Lisa. All the graduate students knew he was leaving his wife for a nineteen-year-old drama student named Sugar Lee.

Lisa opened her notebook and in a dry monotone reported what research attempts she'd tried since the last time they'd met. While he listened, he glanced at a travel brochure about Hawaii.

Finally he interrupted. "Look, don't tell me about your failures. Have you come up with anything positive?"

"Not really. Do you have any suggestions?"

He sighed. "No, just keep at it. Oh, by the way, I won't be in until the tenth of January."

Her mouth dropped open. "What?" she said tensely. "You told me to stay here over the vacation. You said we were going to work on the project together."

"Oh, so I did, didn't I." He put the brochure down. "Hmmm. Well, something's come up. But we'll get together right after school starts in January."

"What am I supposed to do?" she snapped. "I already bought Christmas presents with all the money I was saving for a plane ticket."

"You've got plenty of work to do over the vacation without me. When I come back, we'll get together."

"You're always too busy to see me."

"Look, I'm going to Hawaii on business and I won't be back for three weeks. I'm sorry, but that's the way it is."

"I understand perfectly," she said, staring angrily at him.

"Do you have anything else today?" he asked, glancing impatiently at his watch.

"No," she mumbled, trying to control her anger.

"Can we cut this short then? I've got a million things to do."

Lisa paused at the door.

He looked up. "What are you standing there for?"

She blurted out, "Look, I know it's none of my business, but don't leave your wife and kids for Sugar Lee. Okay, so you're infatuated with her looks, but if you'll just take time to think about what you're doing to your family. Good grief, Dr. Owens, you're at least twenty years older than Sugar Lee. And, good grief, she's such a dummy. I mean, what do you two ever talk about?"

Dr. Owens turned crimson. He stood up. "Worry about your own life, Salinger, not mine! Worry about whether I'll remember this conversation when you take your oral exams. Who are you to tell me what to do? Do you know what you are? You're average, run of the mill. At best you're marginal. I'm not sure I even want my name associated with anything you turn out. I've tried to work with you because I believe women should have equal opportunities, and I've supported the women's movement for years."

"Does that support extend to your wife too, or just to Sugar Lee?"

"Get out!" he yelled.

In the hall she turned off her tape recorder. She decided to save the tape.

Lisa worked steadily on research all week, even spending much of Christmas day stewing over it, trying to fit the pieces together.

Kimberly had gone home with Hal for Christmas, so Lisa was alone. Each day she got up, ate a bowl of Cream of Wheat, put on her jeans and hooded sweatshirt, sat down at her desk, and worked until noon. Then she went to the gym and jogged three miles. After a shower, she ate lunch, then took a nap for a couple of hours before starting to work again, finishing at midnight.

Sometime during that week she realized she was happy to be alone, trying to find the answer to the puzzle of how the universe was put together. But no matter how hard she worked, the equations got worse instead of better. Hundreds of pages of worthless attempts filled her wastepaper basket.

After a week of being alone, wrapped up in her own world of equations representing force fields, hardly ever talking to anyone, she went to church on Sunday. She noticed people were finishing sentences for her. They'd say, "How about this weather?" And she'd stammer, "Yes, it's really . . ." And they'd wait until they could stand the silence no longer, then suggest, "You mean nice?" And she'd slowly nod her head, and they'd leave as fast as they could.

December 29.

She'd worked all day but to no avail. At six o'clock she made herself supper—another can of soup, a packet of Ry-Krisp, two apples, and a cup of coffee. She realized the kitchen was a mess, but it didn't much matter to her.

She ate in the bedroom. Dirty clothes were strewn over the floor, wherever they'd landed when she'd taken them off each night. She looked in her drawer. It was empty. She was out of everything. She'd have to wash clothes before tomorrow.

She filled her laundry bag, went to the basement, put her clothes in a coin-operated washing machine, inserted three quarters, and sat down to wait. It was better not to leave clothes unattended, because they might be stolen.

She was in a tired daze, watching the clothes slosh around, dozing off and then waking up a minute later.

After a while she took her things out of the washer and put them in the dryer.

A girl who lived on the first floor came to wash. To be polite, Lisa said, "How about this weather?"

The girl looked at her. "What about it?"

Lisa didn't know what to say. She hadn't noticed the weather. "I don't know," she finally admitted.

The girl shook her head.

Lisa drowsily stared at the clothes spinning in the dryer, still slipping in and out of consciousness.

Then it happened.

Out of nowhere, on the edge of sleep, she saw a mathematical term jump into place in one of the equations she'd been agonizing over. Suddenly she realized she had the answer that'd eluded Einstein. She knew how to unify all the forces in the universe into one set of equations. She'd found a mathematical quantity that, like a key, opened the universe.

"I've got it," she mumbled, still in a daze. "I never thought I'd get it, but I finally did. Now I've got it."

The girl eyed her suspiciously. "No kidding. It's not contagious, is it?" She moved two chairs away.

"It's so beautiful," Lisa said reverently, her eyes still staring at the clothes bouncing in the dryer while her mind focused on the equations.

The girl looked at where Lisa was looking. "Hey, what are you on?"

Lisa looked around for paper and pencil, but she'd left everything upstairs.

"Do you have any paper?" she asked the girl.

"No, why?"

"I've got to capture it before it leaves."

The girl looked at Lisa's dryer. "It's bolted down—it's not gonna leave."

Lisa opened the dryer and took out two white sheets.

"Do you have a pen or pencil?"

"No."

"Do you have lipstick in your purse?"

"What shade?"

"It doesn't matter."

"Well . . . I usually don't lend it out. You wouldn't believe what some people do to the point."

"Lend me your lipstick!"

"All right, all right. You don't have to shout."

The girl handed it over. Lisa fell to the floor and tried to write on the sheet with it.

"I swear, the weirdos they got in this place . . ."

The lipstick broke in two.

"Somehow I knew you'd do that."

"What else have you got?"

The girl looked through her purse and came up with a Magic Marker. Lisa grabbed it, knelt on the floor, and began writing on the sheet.

"Hey! You just can't go around using people's Magic Markers."

"I have to get it down while it's fresh."

"While what's fresh? The sheet? You don't write on dirty sheets, is that it?"

Lisa kept writing.

"I hope you know that's not going to come out," the girl said.

Lisa filled one sheet and then started on the other. In a few minutes, it was full too. She grabbed a blouse from the dryer and began writing on it. When she finished with that, she looked over at the girl's clothes swishing in the washing machine.

"Oh no, you don't!" The girl pulled her soaking wet clothes out of the washer and ran out of the room.

Lisa grabbed the sheets and blouse and hurried to her apartment. Once inside, she rushed to her desk and began transcribing the equations from the sheets onto paper. The equations proceeded in logical order, each one leading to the other. Tears streamed down her face. The equations revealed order and harmony in the universe.

She thought how surprised Dr. Owens would be—and how he'd apologize for putting her down. But then she pictured him in Hawaii, perhaps at that very moment on the beach rubbing suntan oil on Sugar Lee's back while his ex-wife struggled at home in New Jersey, fighting the snow and the cold.

She decided she didn't want to share her discovery with him. It was too good for him.

She phoned home. "Mom, I've done it!" she burst out when her mother answered.

"You found someone to marry?" her mother asked hopefully.

"Mom, listen to me! I understand how everything fits together."

"What do you mean by everything?"

"The entire universe!"

"That's nice, dear," her mother said pleasantly.

"Mom, you don't understand. I've done something that not even Albert Einstein was able to do."

"Are you sure?" her mother asked. "He was a very smart man. I saw a thing about him on TV."

"I can't describe to you how magnificent it is. I'm just overwhelmed that I should be the one to come up with this."

"Good for you. I'll tell Karen. Oh, before you hang up, do you want any details of her wedding?"

A few minutes later she hung up. She wanted to celebrate. She decided to take a bubble bath and then go out for a pizza.

In a bathtub piled high with suds from Kimberly's bubble bath crystals, Lisa stretched out in the tub, lay back, and relaxed. Her eyes were half closed, but every once in a while she'd giggle with delight.

She'd done it! She'd accomplished what scientists had been trying to do ever since Einstein. She was the one who'd come up with the answer. She'd succeeded where hundreds had failed.

She lifted both arms high over her head in victory and shouted. "All right!" She laughed ecstatically, then laid her head back against the bathroom wall and rested her tired eyes.

She was warm and comfortable and very, very happy.

Another thought lazily drifted into place. Even at this very moment, scientists were still working to discover what she'd just discovered.

Suddenly she sat up, now very much awake. What if somebody came up with her result and published it before she did?

She jumped out of the tub and hastily dried herself. Wrapping the towel around her, she ran to the bedroom and scurried around looking for something to wear. All her clean clothes were downstairs in the dryer. She returned to the bathroom. The clothes she'd taken off before her bath were lying in a sodden heap on the bathroom floor. Finally she ran to the living room, put on the marked-up blouse, then wrapped the two sheets covered with writing around her and pinned them securely. She put on the sheepskin coat and the old pair of bunny slippers she'd had since the seventh grade. She put Kimberly's ski cap over her head because her hair was still wet and she didn't want to catch a cold.

She sat at her desk. She had to get her theory typed up and sent to a science journal before someone beat her to it.

At ten-thirty that night, Kimberly returned from her vacation trip. "All right, what's been going on here?"

"I can't talk to you now," Lisa said, typing away.

"What're you wearing under that coat?"

"Two sheets."

"Bed sheets? Let me look. Good grief, there's strange writing all over them. You wrote on your sheets. Why would anyone do that?"

No answer.

Kimberly cocked her head sideways. "Why can't I read a word of it?"

"It's Greek symbols. I put 'em on with a Magic Marker."

She frowned. "So—you wrote Greek on your bed sheets and then dressed up in them?"

No answer from Lisa.

"Why?" she asked calmly.

"I can't explain now."

"Answer me this—were you alone when you wrote on your sheets?"

"Of course I was alone!"

"All right, don't get mad—I'm just trying to recreate how it was. Okay, you're sitting around, all alone, when suddenly you think, 'Gee, I think I'll go get a Magic Marker and write strange Greek symbols all over my bed sheets, and then I'll wrap the Magic Sheets around me, pin 'em up, and wear 'em.' And I bet that was so much fun that you decided to pull my ski cap over your face, and to wear those silly little bunny slippers you've hung onto since you were a little girl. Is that the way it was?" She paused, then continued. "I'm your friend, and I understand how a person could become, shall we say, temporarily unstable, especially if that person was all alone over Christmas. But there's one thing I've got to know. Please tell me you haven't gone outside like that."

No answer.

"Lisa, have you ever had any professional counseling for this—this little problem of yours?"

"I can't talk now."

"I give up. You're really strange."

Kimberly walked into the kitchen and then came right back out. "I guess you know the kitchen is absolutely disgusting. Didn't you ever take health in high school?"

"I'm too busy to talk to you now."

She wandered into the bedroom, screamed, and came running out again. "What have you been doing in there? There're thousands of dead spiders on the floor!"

"No there aren't—I just dropped a plate of wheat sprouts a few days ago, and I never cleaned it up."

Kimberly shook her head. "You are so weird! Look, I'll make a deal with you. Get out of your Greek sheets, put on some real clothes, help me clean up this place—

and I won't tell anyone about what you've been doing while I've been away."

"All my clothes are downstairs in the dryer."

Next Kimberly tried to be a calm voice of reason. She spoke very slowly. "Then what you need to do is go down and get them from the dryer, and then you'll have them to wear."

Lisa kept typing. "I'm too busy."

"Too busy to get your clothes? Believe me, nobody is that busy!"

"I can't talk to you."

"Look, Hal's waiting in the hall. He wants to come in and listen to a record he got me for Christmas. It's a new group called the Cardiac Arrest."

"I'm not moving."

"Well, aren't we in a rotten mood!"

"Don't talk."

"I'll talk if I want—this is a free country."

Hal knocked on the door. Kimberly opened it. They gossiped for a few minutes, then Hal left. She came back. "Hal's gone for a pizza. When he comes back, we're going to listen to my record. I think you should get dressed and throw away all the garbage you've scattered around the place. I'll help you, and when we're all through, you can have some pizza with us."

"I'm not moving till I've finished."

"How long will that be?"

"It might take all night."

Kimberly slammed a bowl of limp sprouts down on the end table. "Go ahead then—stay crazy! But I'm letting Hal in, and he's going to see you, and then he's gonna go out and tell the whole campus how spooky you are!" She fought to stay calm. "So if you don't want him to see you this way . . ."

"I'm not moving."

Kimberly stormed off to the kitchen and then came right back, yelling. "If anybody wants to start a mold museum, tell 'em they can start here!"

She stayed in the kitchen for only a short time before storming back out again. "The least you can do is get decent for Hal."

"I am decent."

"Wearing bed sheets is not decent."

"It's a blouse, then two sheets and a coat. Besides, who are you to talk to me about being decent? I'm completely covered, which is more than we can say about you in that red dress you wore last month."

Kimberly paused, then said, "All right, I'll admit you're decent."

"Fine." Lisa started to work again.

"Decent yes, but let's face it—very, very tacky. Extremely tacky. The sheet's bad enough—but a grown person wearing bunny slippers? How many college students in the United States do you suppose still wear bunny slippers?"

Lisa whirled around. "Can't you see I'm busy?"

"Yes, I can see that! But why are you so busy? I don't understand that. This is Christmas break."

"I know you don't understand!" Lisa shouted back.

That infuriated Kimberly. "Is that right? Well, listen to me, I understand a good deal more than you give me credit for. At least I've never written on my bed sheets with a Magic Marker! And I'm smart enough not to leave soup on simmer in a covered pan for a week. Good grief, Lisa, I hope you know it's fermented. I took it off the stove fifteen minutes ago and it's still bubbling. Go ahead, tell me why you're so busy. Believe me, I'll understand."

"All right, I'll tell you! I've just discovered the Secret of the Universe."

Kimberly threw up her hands. "Oh sure! And I'm Joan of Arc."

Hal knocked on the door. She went to answer it. He came in. "I got something new. It's called Chinese pizza. Hi, Lisa. Going to a toga party?"

"Ignore her," Kimberly said.

"Sure thing."

Kimberly brought in some plates and a bottle of wine. Hal opened the pizza container, and a rich smell filled the room. Kimberly put on the Cardiac Arrest record and turned the volume up, trying to drive Lisa to the storeroom. The record sounded like someone kicking a set of drums down the steps of the Washington Monument.

"Turn it down!" Lisa yelled.

"It's my apartment too, you know."

Lisa suffered through one more song, then jumped up and broke the record in two with her bare hands.

"That was my Christmas present from Hal you just destroyed!"

"I'll pay for it! Believe me, it was worth it." She tossed her purse at Kimberly and sat down again.

"What's wrong with her?" Hal asked.

"Who knows? She gets spookier by the day. Did I tell you she talks to mice now when she's in the storeroom?"

Lisa kept typing.

Kimberly continued. "She could be attractive and popular, like me, but no, she doesn't try. And her clothes—why does she always have to look like a refugee? And why does she only wear drab colors?"

"Beats me. Why's she so paranoid tonight?"

"Listen to this," Kimberly grumbled. "She says she's come up with the secret of the universe. Whatever it is, it can't be important enough to sit in front of us wearing two bed sheets marked all over with Magic Marker, a ski cap, and those infantile slippers. And the mess she left the bathroom in—I'd be embarrassed for you to see it. Not to mention the fact she used up an entire bottle of my bubble bath."

"She's found the secret of the universe?" Hal said. "That could be important. Did she say what it is?"

"Of course not. Even if she did, who'd ever understand a word she'd say?"

Hal rubbed his chin thoughtfully. "You know what I

think the secret of the universe is? I think it's this—go with the flow, stay loose, and look for opportunities. There's opportunities all around, sometimes under our very noses. Take the dimpled golf ball, for instance. Did you know they used to make golf balls perfectly round, but in a tournament the pro golfers would use all their old knicked-up balls because they found out they traveled farther? And then one guy started making them dimpled. Now there was an opportunity right under somebody's nose, but just one person saw it. It's something to think about, right?"

Lisa heard them talking but couldn't stop to react. She had to keep working. Suddenly she sneezed. She jumped up, ran to the refrigerator, pulled out a carton of yogurt, dumped the contents into a glass, poured milk over it, stirred it, picked up an empty glass, returned to her desk, took a mouthful of yogurt, gargled, and spit into the other glass.

"Good grief, what is she doing?" Hal asked.

"Gargling yogurt," Kimberly said. "She does it whenever she thinks she's getting sick—but watching her do it makes me sick."

"Does she always wear that coat to bed?"

"Every night since November."

"Sheepskin pajamas," Hal said. "That's got to be a first. I wonder why. Must be some deep-seated psychological need—like maybe she has a crush on the Marlboro man."

Lisa turned around and yelled, "Would you two shut up?"

"Sorry, your highness," Kimberly said sarcastically.

A few minutes later, the pizza and wine were gone. Hal started for the bathroom, but Kimberly stopped him and made him wait until she cleaned it up.

While he waited, he stood over Lisa and watched. "What are all those little squiggles on the paper for?"

She turned to glare at him.

He shrugged his shoulders. "Just asking—no need to

get mad. You think you're so great, don't you. Well look, I'm smart too. Oh sure, I'm not into mathematics like you are. I'm more philosophical. Did I ever tell you my philosophy of life? I got it from seeing *South Pacific*. It's this: 'Happy thoughts, keep thinking happy thoughts, think about things you'd like to do. You gotta have a dream, if you don't have a dream, how you gonna make a dream come true?' That's it. That's my philosophy of life."

Kimberly came out of the bathroom. "It's okay to use now," she said. He left.

Kimberly put the pizza container in the garbage, then returned. "Are you almost through?"

"No," Lisa said.

"How much longer is it gonna be?"

"It might be all night."

Hal returned a minute later.

"How am I supposed to sleep with her banging away on that typewriter all night?" Kimberly complained.

"Hey, Lisa," Hal said, "if it'll help out, I'll move the typewriter down to the storeroom for you. Then you can be with Mickey Mouse and all your other little friends."

Lisa stood up and shouted, pointing to the door, "The both of you—get out of here!"

"You see what I put up with?" Kimberly complained.

Lisa ran to her purse and took all the money she had and gave it to Kimberly. "Take it! Just get out! Go to a movie or go bowling or to an arcade—just get out of here and let me work!"

"We don't want your money," Kimberly said self-righteously.

"Hey, wait a minute," Hal said. "Let's not be hasty. How much did she give you?"

Kimberly counted. "Thirty-seven dollars and fifty-four cents."

He reached for the money. "Well, if she offered it, I say let's take it."

They left with the money.

C H A P T E R   T W O

The night slipped by. Lisa finished the first draft, then started on the second. When she finished that, she went through every equation again to make sure there were no errors. Then she typed the final version. By the time she was finally done, it was six-thirty in the morning.

All that remained to do was the title page. She tried several, then decided on "THE DESCRIPTION OF ALL THE FORCES IN THE UNIVERSE IN TERMS OF A GRAND UNIFIED FIELD THEORY."

For the author of the paper, she first tried *by Lisa Salinger and James Owens, Princeton University.* But then she wondered if an editor might discount the paper because it was written by a woman. Also, the name Lisa seemed too folksy for the most important result in physics in the last half of the twentieth century. She changed it to *L. Salinger and J. Owens, Princeton University.*

Then she pictured Dr. Owens and Sugar in Hawaii strolling on the beach together. Hadn't he said he didn't want his name on any paper she'd write?

She retyped the title page to read *by L. Salinger, Princeton University.*

Seven o'clock—one hour until the post office opened. She went to the kitchen and opened a can of soup and ate it cold out of the can. While she ate, she stood beside her desk and read what she'd written. It was good.

At seven-thirty, she put the manuscript into an envelope and sealed it, then went downstairs to get her clothes from the dryer. She was still wearing the sheets and slippers.

While she was there the girl from the night before came in to finish her laundry. She took one look at Lisa in the sheet, swore, then said, "That's it. I'm moving back on campus."

Upstairs in her apartment Lisa threw the clean clothes on her bed, then picked through the pile to find what she needed to get dressed. While she dressed, she noticed orange splotches on her body from wearing the marked sheet. Ten minutes later, wearing jeans and a hooded sweatshirt, she looked in the mirror. A few orange marks were still visible on her neck.

At eight o'clock she put on her down-filled parka and jogged to the post office. She imagined a distinguished-looking scientist somewhere with his version of her theory putting his manuscript into an envelope and driving leisurely to the post office near his home. She had to beat him.

When she got to the post office, she looked in her purse and remembered she'd given all her money to Kimberly.

No problem, she thought. *I'll cash a check.*

She got in line. In a few minutes, it was her turn. "I need to write a check so I can Xerox something and then mail it."

"We don't accept checks."

"The post office in Fargo, North Dakota, accepts checks."

"Then I suggest you go there. Next?"

"It's just for five dollars."

"Sorry. Next."

"Look, this is very important. I've got to mail this right away."

"Next."

She wandered around the post office, trying to decide what to do. She imagined the distinguished-looking scientist dropping his manuscript into a mail chute. He was going to beat her out unless she did something fast.

She walked up to a man who'd just come in.

"Excuse me. I need five dollars."

"What for?"

"I have to send a paper I wrote to a science journal, and I don't have any money because I gave it all to my roommate and her boyfriend to get them out of the apartment last night so I could finish writing it."

The man laughed and walked away.

A woman came in. Lisa approached her. "I need five dollars. I'll pay you back."

The woman glared at her. "Are you a student?"

"Yes, I am."

"You ought to be ashamed of yourself for panhandling."

Lisa smiled. "It was just a joke. I'm pledging a sorority, and they made me do it."

The woman smiled. "Of course." She walked away.

More people came in. Lisa began sizing them up, looking for an easy touch.

She walked up to a sincere-looking man. "I need five dollars to get food for my baby."

"You have a baby?"

"Yes. Please help me. My husband left me, and there's no food. Please, just a few dollars'll buy formula for my baby."

"Why don't you get a job?"

"I have a rare disease." Lisa showed him her orange-splotched neck.

"Oh, that looks bad," the man said, backing away.

He stopped and reached in his wallet.

"Is the baby all right?"

"So far he is—if I can just get him some medicine too."

"Of course." He gave her ten dollars.

Lisa took the money. "Give me your name, and I'll return the money to you in a couple of days."

She took the money, ran across the street, and waited for him to leave the post office. As soon as he did, she ran back, got change, and Xeroxed her manuscript.

Five minutes later her article was on its way to the editorial office of *Physical Review Letters*.

As she leisurely walked back to her apartment, she smiled and thought about her panhandling in the post office. For a minute someone believed she really did have a child who needed food.

Where was her husband? He worked for the CIA and was away on a dangerous mission. He was ruggedly handsome and yet sensitive too. How had she met him? He'd seen her at a party. He'd been attracted to her from the start. "I love your dress," he'd said. "You look so good in gray."

Those were his very words.

She found it strangely exciting to be someone else.

A month after the new semester began, she received a letter from *Physical Review Letters* containing several suggestions for improving the manuscript. It took her a week to revise it; then she sent it off again. Two weeks later she was advised the paper had been accepted for publication. Because of the importance of her work, they were going to move up the publication date.

There were no more research meetings with Dr. Owens. He ignored her and she avoided him. The rumor on campus was that the divorce was final and that he'd moved in with Sugar Lee.

Her paper was published in May. The day it came out, Dr. Owens and the chairman of the Physics Department, Dr. Remick, burst into a class she was attending and demanded to see her privately. When they got in the hall, Dr. Owens pointed to the article she'd written. "What is the meaning of this?" he snapped.

"Oh, that's just a paper I wrote over Christmas break."

"You had no right to submit this without my approval!" he protested. "We should've worked it out together and then submitted it with my name listed as co-author."

"You didn't do anything on it. And if you'll remember, you said you didn't want your name on any paper I'd write. Besides, I wanted to get it published before anyone else beat me to it. If you'll recall, you weren't available over Christmas."

"And you didn't have the common courtesy to wait till I got back?"

"I was afraid someone'd get it published before I did."

"You've embarrassed Princeton in front of the whole world."

"Why's that?"

"Because it has Princeton's name on it, that's why," he grumbled. "Besides that, your whole approach is ridiculous."

"The people who reviewed it didn't think so," she said.

Dr. Owens leaned into her. "Apparently you don't understand the ethics of university research. I'm filing a complaint with the graduate dean. When I'm through with you, young lady, you'll be lucky to still be in school."

Dr. Remick added, "This is very serious. We're having a staff meeting today to decide what to do. I'd like you to wait in another room in case we need to speak to you."

During the meeting, she was forced to sit in an office next door, like a naughty child awaiting punishment. An hour later, Dr. Remick came to see her. "We want you to send a letter to the editor, stating that the paper was sent prematurely and that it's currently undergoing revision, under the direction of Dr. Owens. Then when it's resubmitted for publication, we'd like it to have Dr. Owens's name as a co-author."

"The paper doesn't need revision," she said.

"Your scholarship hangs in the balance. And unless you cooperate, we'll have no choice but to terminate you as a student."

"I'll think about it. Give me a little time."

"All right. See me tomorrow morning at eight o'clock sharp."

That night on the Johnny Carson show, a famous astronomer was a guest. "Johnny, you might be interested that a search for unity in the universe, which has been going on since man first looked into the night sky, might be over. Recently a paper was published by a physicist at Princeton that shows that all the forces in the universe can be represented by one set of equations. If the theory proves correct, then we will, for the first time, be able to say that we really do understand the universe in which we live."

"Who came up with this theory?"

"I can't remember the name, but if he's from Princeton, he must be very good."

Johnny grinned. "I'd like to meet him. If he understands the universe, maybe he can help me find a place to park in the NBC lot."

The next morning when she entered the physics building, she noticed a TV crew standing in the hall near the graduate carrels.

The interviewer walked up to her. "One of the students says you're L. Salinger."

"Yes."

"You're a woman," he said.

She stared back at him. "That's right."

As he interviewed her on camera, a crowd of graduate students and faculty began to gather.

"As I understand it, what you've done is to bring harmony to the universe. Is that right?"

"Well, in a mathematical sense, that's true. I've developed a set of interlocking equations that unify all the forces in the universe. All that we see, from the very small to the very large, is now part of an elegant pattern predicted by these equations."

"Is it true that Einstein spent many years of his life searching for the very thing you've come up with?"

She smiled. "Yes, that's true."

"Where exactly were you when you made your discovery?"

"I was in a laundry room washing clothes."

"A laundry room?"

"That's right. I was watching the clothes bounce around in the dryer. I guess I dozed off, and when I woke up I had the answer."

"I hope you don't mind me saying this, but you look too young to be the successor to Albert Einstein."

"Well, Einstein was only twenty-eight years old when he came up with his theory of relativity."

"And how old are you?"

"I'm twenty-one."

"I notice you brought a sack with you this morning. What's in the sack?"

"My lunch."

"And what does the successor to Einstein have for lunch?"

She shrugged. "I really don't think anyone cares about that."

"I think you'll find people will want to know a great deal about you now."

She started pulling things out of the sack. "Well, for lunch I always have an apple . . . and some yogurt . . . and in this Tupperware container is my wheat and alfalfa sprouts." She pulled out what looked like a bird's nest.

"You eat that for lunch?" the interviewer asked.

"Oh yes. Every day."

"I see. Tell me, is there a man in your life?"

"No."

"If there was one, I wonder what he'd think about

your discovery. How does a man deal with a woman who's smarter than Albert Einstein?"

"I can't answer that question."

"Dr. Salinger . . ."

Out of the corner of her eye, she saw Dr. Owens come to the edge of the crowd.

"I'm not really a doctor. I'm a graduate student."

"What can we call you then?" the interviewer asked.

"Lisa, I guess."

"Lisa, is there anyone who should share in your discovery?"

"Well, in a discovery like this, one always stands on the shoulders of giants. There's been much work done previously that helped me arrive at my equations."

"Is there anyone here at Princeton you would consider directly responsible for helping make possible your discovery?"

She paused. "Well yes, there really is." She glanced over to Dr. Owens, who was self-consciously straightening his tie.

"And who might that be?"

She could feel the anticipation of the faculty.

"Sugar Lee."

Dr. Owens stormed away.

A few minutes later the faculty began another emergency session.

An hour later Dr. Remick visited her again. "You've got to give Dr. Owens some credit for your work."

"Why? He said the paper's wrong."

"We went over your paper carefully in our meeting. It may have some merit, although we still maintain it could have been greatly improved if you'd only worked with us on it."

"I like it the way it is."

"What's wrong with you?" he asked impatiently.

"Dr. Owens didn't have anything to do with what I put in that paper. He was off frolicking on the beach with his Sugar Baby while his wife and family struggled through the worst Christmas of their lives. It's the same thing my father did to our family. Dr. Owens deserted his family. Why should I reward him for that?"

"That's a personal matter. We can't have graduate students publishing independently."

"I won't anymore."

"We'll give you two days to think about it, and then you're through here."

She spent the rest of the day in the library. As she walked home for supper, she noticed a van from a TV station outside the apartment. Through the open door of her apartment, she saw a woman interviewing Kimberly. She continued walking quietly past her apartment to the storeroom, where she lay down on the cot. She looked at a large cobweb in the corner and listened to the sounds of people in apartments preparing supper.

She fell asleep.

Suddenly the door opened. "And this is the storeroom where she sometimes works," Kimberly announced cheerily. Bright lights flooded the room. Lisa sat up and faced a TV camera.

"Oh, here she is now," Kimberly said proudly.

"Dr. Salinger, could we have a word with you?"

A woman sat beside her on the cot and touched her on the shoulder. "We're so proud of you!"

Lisa yawned. "Who is?"

"The women of America. We want to thank you for showing that a woman can be as great a genius as any man."

"You're welcome," she mumbled, still not quite awake.

"Your roommate says you come here sometimes. Exactly why do you spend time here?" The camera loomed above them.

Kimberly, off-camera, vigorously shook her head, mouthing the words *my mother.*

Lisa understood. "I come here to meditate," she said.

"And does it help to be here among all this?" The

camera panned the suitcases and trunks and ancient
ironing boards and broken bicycles.

"Oh, yes, it matches the Karma of the universe," Lisa
said, intentionally sounding mysterious.

"Do you think it significant that a woman should
come up with a theory that dwarfs what even Albert Einstein did?"

She paused. "I don't understand the question."

"In light of the women's movement, I mean."

"The universe has no gender," Lisa said.

The interviewer started to gush. "*The universe has no
gender.* That is *so* profound. I know you're going to be an
inspiration to every woman in America who aspires to
greatness. You may not know it now, but you're going to
be a symbol to women everywhere. Lisa, what would you
like to say to the sixty million people who will watch this?"

"Sixty million people?" She nervously tried to adjust
her hair with her fingers.

The woman stopped her. "It's okay, you're fine the
way you are. Lisa, what do you have to say to the house-
wife in Schenectady, to the flight attendant in Los
Angeles, to the business woman on her way home in New
York City, to the teenager studying around the TV . . .
what would you like to say to the women of America?"

"Well, uh, I don't know. I mean, I guess I'd say . . .
hang in there . . ."

"Lisa, do you have a philosophy of life?"

"A philosophy of life?" she stammered.

"Yes."

She nervously bit her lip. "Well, sure, I guess so."

"Tell us what it is."

"Well . . . I guess it's . . ." She paused, trying desper-
ately to think of something. "Well, it's . . . You gotta have
a dream, if you don't have a dream, how you gonna make
a dream come true?"

The interviewer hugged her. "*You gotta have a
dream*—what a message of hope. I want to thank you for

showing us what we can become. You've given us hope, and, as a woman I'd like to thank you from the bottom of my heart."

"Okay, sure, you bet," Lisa said.

The phone rang all night. Lisa had an offer from the American Yogurt Institute to do TV commercials. She had a call from Phil Donahue's staff inviting her to appear on his show. She was invited to give a paper at the meeting of the American Physical Society next month. Two writers called and offered to do her life story.

Hal sat and watched all this happening. "We're sitting on a gold mine! This is definitely bigger than dimpled golf balls."

At eleven-thirty, the vice-president of Princeton called. "I strongly suggest that you credit Dr. Owens as your co-author."

"I won't do it. He didn't help me write the paper."

"Get yourself a good lawyer then."

"Why?"

"Tonight Dr. Owens showed me proof that you stole his ideas and published them as your own. He's willing to carry this through the courts. You'll need a lawyer."

"I can't afford a lawyer."

"Then cooperate with Dr. Owens. Is it so much to ask for you to include him as a co-author?"

"Yes, it is. It's not his paper. He didn't have a thing to do with it. And why did he wait until now to say they were his equations?"

"He said he was trying to protect you, but now that he sees you mean to take full credit for it, he has to protect his rights."

"He's lying!"

"That will be for the ethics committee to decide. We're having a hearing next week."

CHAPTER THREE

T he next week in *Time* and *Newsweek,* the controversy between Lisa and Dr. Owens was discussed. But the disagreement really came to a head at the ethics committee meeting, which the major news networks covered.

Dr. Owens was called as a witness. He showed a November entry in his notebook containing Lisa's equations.

"Dr. Owens," a member of the ethics committee asked politely, "what you're saying is that Ms. Salinger took your equations and published them as her own."

"Yes, I'm afraid that's exactly what she did."

Lisa jumped up. "That's a bold-faced lie!"

"Ms. Salinger, please sit down. You'll have your chance later." He turned to Dr. Owens. "How would she get access to these equations?"

"We talked about them in our weekly research meetings."

"And so she knew about your equations as early as November?"

"That's right. My intention was that we'd work on them together and get the bugs out, so to speak, before sending a paper off for publication. But she must've seen their value and gone ahead, trying to claim all the credit for herself. In a way I feel sorry for her. She's young, and she made a mistake in judgment. I hold nothing against her personally. I just want the record set straight about where the equations actually came from."

Lisa gritted her teeth.

She was called next.

"Ms. Salinger, you claim the ideas in your paper were completely original with you, and that Dr. Owens had no part in them?"

"That's right."

"But you just saw the equations in his research notebook, dated November 4 of last year."

"Yes."

"How do you explain that?"

"Simple—he copied them in his notebook after my paper came out."

"That's a serious accusation. Did Dr. Owens ever discuss these equations with you in your research meetings?"

"Of course not."

"I see. Was there anyone else in those meetings besides the two of you?"

"No."

"Dr. Owens has a fine record here at Princeton. It's hard for me to believe he'd resort to something as unethical as you're suggesting. How will we ever be able to decide if your allegation is true?"

Lisa paused. "I haven't told anyone about this before, but the fact is I tape recorded all our research meetings."

Dr. Owens momentarily winced but then recovered. "She's lying—she never taped anything."

"How could you tape a meeting without Dr. Owens knowing?"

Lisa picked up the book in her lap and opened it to show the hidden tape recorder.

Dr. Owens and his lawyer had a private conference. A reporter for the *New York Times* ran out to phone her newspaper. Lisa looked vacantly into the TV camera and smiled smugly in what was later described as a Mona Lisa look—very understated.

Dr. Owens's lawyer stood up. "We can't allow the playing of any tape-recorded evidence until it's first been verified by audio experts that the tape has not been altered by Ms. Salinger. A test like that might take several months."

The ethics committee members stared at each other, at a loss to know what to do.

Lisa didn't wait—she started the tape running. It was Dr. Owens's voice. "Have you come up with anything positive?"

"Not really. Do you have any suggestions?"

"No, just keep at it."

As the tape played, Dr. Owens's lawyer complained loudly. It was difficult to hear anything over the noise. Lisa backed the tape up again, placed the recorder next to a microphone, and started it over again. Now it bellowed out across the room.

Dr. Owens's lawyer shouted, "If you allow her to play this, we'll bring a lawsuit against each member of this committee for defamation of character."

The chairman gave up. "Ms. Salinger, turn off the tape please."

Lisa shouted, "What's wrong with you people? You said you wanted proof. Well, here it is. Listen to it!"

The chairman, realizing that Princeton now had a scandal being covered by the networks, suddenly turned on her. "You're out of order! Please return to your seat."

She blew up. "What do you mean, I'm out of order?" She pointed an accusing finger at Dr. Owens. "He's accused me of lying and cheating and being dishonest! But that's exactly what he's done! And I've got proof! So why am I out of order?"

Dr. Owens's lawyer protested. "She's already said enough for us to sue her. If you want to protect her, as well as this committee, from further lawsuits, as well as save Princeton further embarrassment, I suggest you dismiss this hearing immediately. This matter should be tried in a court of law, not in an ethics committee meeting."

The chairman declared the meeting closed.

"WHY AREN'T THERE ANY WOMEN ON THIS COMMITTEE?" Lisa raged.

That week Lisa Salinger and Sugar Lee made the cover of *National Enquirer*. Sugar was shown posing in her dancing leotards, while Lisa was pictured shouting at the committee chairman. The article was titled "The Restless Women in Dr. Owens's Life."

During the summer Lisa tried to resume her graduate studies, but it was nearly impossible.

The faculty, still angry about Dr. Owens being humiliated, treated her with icy scorn. No matter what she did, it was wrong. If she tried to be inconspicuous, they told her they expected more from her. When she became assertive, they interpreted it as an attempt to undermine their position as professors. Every physics question she asked in class sent fear through her teachers, since they assumed she knew the answer and was only trying to trap them.

Advised by his attorney that the best defense is a good offense, Dr. Owens brought a lawsuit against Lisa for defamation of character. That meant she had to get herself a lawyer. Her lawyer, a woman, suggested that Lisa initiate a countersuit against Dr. Owens. The tape was sent to a lab in Washington, D.C., to be analyzed.

As long as the case pended, Dr. Owens's job and reputation were preserved. Therefore, to Lisa the case seemed to drag on forever. In order to pay for the ever-mounting legal fees, she was forced to go on the lecture circuit on weekends, much to the delight of Hal and Kimberly, who began functioning as her agents.

As much as she disliked Hal, Lisa found him a good

manager of money. Most of all, with him and Kimberly helping, she didn't have to worry about any travel or business details.

She spoke nearly every weekend. Because of her accomplishments in science and also the publicity resulting from the Salinger-Owens confrontation, she spoke to many feminist groups throughout the country.

Because of Hal's eagerness for them to get the forty thousand dollars she had been offered, she became the TV spokesperson for yogurt, doing three sixty-second spots for national TV.

Hal and Kimberly kept on the lookout for peripheral money-making concepts. "We've contacted the Mattel people about a Lisa doll," Kimberly reported one day as the three of them rode a plane to Chicago, where Lisa was scheduled to speak. "They like the concept—it'll be the industry's first feminist doll. They figure it'll start a whole new trend. Barbie dolls are out anyway—they're sexist, and besides, nobody looks like that anyway. With the Lisa doll, the clothes aren't that splashy, but where they'll make their money is in Phase Two sales—the Lisa doll traveling in a space shuttle, the Lisa doll presiding over a corporate board meeting, the Lisa doll picketing a nuclear reactor, the Lisa doll sitting in the oval office. What do you think?"

She looked up from a physics paper she was writing. "I don't care. Do anything you want—just don't bother me about it."

Hal grinned. "We're talking big bucks here, kid. Just stick with us, and we'll make you rich."

"How about this?" Kimberly said. "A designer dress with your equations on it."

"Sure, whatever you say," she mumbled, wishing she were already in her hotel room so she could be alone to work.

"If you'd like, we can have it done in gray for you," Kimberly said.

The auditorium was filled with ten thousand women. Lisa stood in the wings waiting to be introduced. Hal and Kimberly were next to her.

"Just read it the way I wrote it, and you won't have any trouble," Kimberly said.

They heard the introduction booming over the auditorium. "Our next speaker needs no introduction. She's a distinguished scientist. She recently published a landmark paper in which she unified all the forces in the universe into one set of equations. Not only has she contributed to science, she is also becoming a leading spokesperson for the women's movement. It was she who first coined the now famous line 'The universe has no gender.' It is now my pleasure to introduce the recently named winner of the American Physical Society's Halverson-Smith Award for outstanding theoretical research, Ms. Lisa Salinger."

They gave her a standing ovation as she walked onstage.

"You're all very kind," she said when the noise died down. "It's wonderful to be here and feel your warmth and love, and to know that in a real sense, whether we come from north or south, east or west, we are all sisters . . .

"The human mind escapes any efforts to be limited. Any human mind is a national resource, and the minds and courage of women everywhere must be recognized for the great potential we possess to alter the world in which we live. Excellence, like the universe, has no gender."

She continued for several minutes.

". . . In conclusion, let me close with something that has meant a great deal to me. During those dark days when I wrestled to find the secret of the forces in the universe, this thought buoyed me up. It's from the musical *South Pacific*. It goes like this, 'Happy thoughts, keep thinking happy thoughts, think about things you'd like to do. You gotta have a dream, if you don't got a dream, how you gonna make a dream come true?' Thank you very much."

She started offstage, but the applause was deafening. She paused and lifted up her arms into a V. The image was captured by Hal and Kimberly. They made plans to market it on T-shirts.

At the January meeting of the American Physical Society she chaired a session dealing with the Salinger theory. During that same meeting she proposed several experiments that might be used to validate her theory.

In May the lawsuit between her and Dr. Owens finally went to court. The trial made national news. Dr. Owens's lawyers managed to have Lisa's tape thrown out as evidence. The only thing that saved her was the appearance of the girl who'd loaned her a Magic Marker in the laundry room, as well as Hal and Kimberly's testimony.

In the end Lisa's name was cleared of all charges. The next day Dr. Owens's lawyer called to ask if Lisa's countersuit might be settled out of court. Dr. Owens and Lisa, along with their lawyers, scheduled a meeting.

"I've just been fired at Princeton," Dr. Owens said bitterly. "Sugar left me to go to California because a movie producer saw her picture in the *National Enquirer* and wants to make her a star. My ex-wife won't talk to me, and my kids hate me. So what else do you want from me?"

"Five hundred thousand dollars," she said coolly.

He blanched.

His lawyer cleared his throat. "My client has no income and no assets. I think you're being unreasonable."

"Maybe you're right," Lisa said. "Tell you what—I'm such an old softie, I'll settle for two hundred and fifty thousand dollars."

She enjoyed watching Dr. Owens squirm. But ten minutes later, she realized how tired she was of legal battles, and she dropped all legal action against Dr. Owens.

In June a physicist from Japan who two years earlier had won a Nobel Prize published a paper reporting experimental results that agreed with predictions made from Lisa's theory. A few days later she was named a recipient of the Sullivan Award from the American Association for the Advancement of Science.

One morning she was wakened by a bright flash of light. She looked up to see Kimberly standing over her with a camera.

"What are you doing?" Lisa complained.

"I'm taking a class in photography, and I needed to take some pictures. You looked so cute there sleeping. I hope you don't mind."

"I mind, Kimberly. You woke me up."

"Sorry."

A few days later she was in her robe eating breakfast. Kimberly called out her name. She turned around and Kimberly took another picture.

For the next week every time she turned around, Kimberly was taking a picture.

The last straw was when she sat on the edge of the bathtub, her hair dripping wet, wearing a tattered bathrobe, clipping her toenails. Kimberly opened the door and took a picture.

"Kimberly, that's it! Any more pictures and I'm breaking your camera!"

"That was the last one—I promise."

Two months later, in August, Brent Peters, a graduate student, approached her as she studied in the library. "Hey, how's our cover girl?" he asked.

"What?"

He tossed a copy of *People* magazine on her desk. There, on the cover, was Lisa Salinger mopping the kitchen floor. Below the picture it read, "The Woman Who Topped Einstein: A Fascinating Account by Her Roommate."

Self-consciously she placed a textbook over the magazine to cover up her picture.

He laughed. "I'm afraid that won't do the trick. There's thousands of copies on newsstands all over the country."

She stared in shock at her picture.

"The article's not so bad," he said. "I'll show you— okay?"

She grimly nodded her head.

He opened the magazine to the first picture, showing her asleep on the cot in the storeroom. The caption read: "Lisa often comes to the storeroom and meditates. Sometimes she talks to mice. (The mice are not shown.)"

The second picture showed the broken Cardiac Arrest record. "When she's working, she has a violent temper. Once when I had a few friends in for popcorn after a basketball game, Lisa stomped in, broke the record we were playing, then marched back to the storeroom. I guess she prefers the company of mice."

The third picture was of the bed sheets covered with equations. The caption began, "In coming up with her theory, she first wrote her equations on two sheets, then wore them for days at a time. Nobody knows why she did this."

The fourth picture showed Lisa wearing her sheepskin coat. "She wears this coat to bed when it's cold."

The fifth picture looked as if she had a bird's nest in her mouth. The caption read: "Lisa likes health food. This is what it's like sitting across from her at supper."

Lisa closed the magazine. Tears ran down her cheeks.

"Hey, take it easy," Brent said. "It's not the end of the world. In seven days, there'll be another issue, and nobody'll remember you anymore."

He reached out and took her hand. "Hey, cheer up.

How about if I take you out for a movie tonight? It'd give us both a chance to relax. How about it?"

He seemed sincere. She gratefully accepted the invitation.

After the movie he took her to his place to show her his computer. She sat down and turned it on.

"Would you like a drink?" he asked.

"Just some coffee, if you have any."

"You sure you don't want any wine?"

"No, thanks."

He put on soft music. In a few minutes he returned with her coffee. He sat next to her and tried to put his arm around her. She moved away.

He smiled. "Hey, loosen up, girl. Don't be so tense."

"I don't like a guy to assume I'm his property just because I go out with him once."

"I understand. Hey look, Lisa, I've been watching you for quite a while. You know, you really are pretty. Hey, how about looking at me when I talk? Here, let me turn this off." He turned off the computer. "That's better. Now come over and sit down and let's talk."

"I'd rather talk here."

"Lisa, do you ever get lonely?"

She jumped up. "I really have to go home now."

"What's your hurry? Answer my question—do you ever get lonely?"

"Sure, so what?"

"There's no point in both of us being lonely, is there?"

"Do you have a phone? I need to call a taxi."

"Don't go. I won't bite you."

"You make me nervous."

"Hey, relax. Sit down. We'll talk physics. I'll stay clear over here."

She sat down again.

"I need some help," he said.

"With what?"

"I flunked my graduate comprehensive exam."

"Okay, I'll help you study for it next time."

"That's not what I had in mind. I was just a few points below passing. Talk the department into saying I passed."

"How?"

"Threaten to leave if they don't pass me. You're important now, because of all the good publicity you're giving the department. Everyone wants to go to Princeton because of you. The administration doesn't want you to go someplace else. Look, all I'm asking is just to mention that you'd be unhappy if I wasn't allowed to continue toward my Ph.D."

"Is that the reason you asked me out tonight?"

"Of course not. I just want us to be good friends."

"I'm sorry, but I can't ask them to pass you."

He tried to kiss her, but she pulled away. "No."

He stopped acting. "All right. Forget it. I'll get your coat."

A minute later he tossed the coat on the couch. "The phone's over there," he said. "Call yourself a taxi."

"Our friendship's over so soon?" she asked sarcastically.

"What did you expect? You think anybody's gonna be nice to you now unless they want something? Face it, Lisa, you're a commodity now, like toothpaste. You're billed as the next Einstein. That's going to haunt you for the rest of your life. Get used to people exploiting you."

She phoned for a cab, then put on her coat.

"Don't go away feeling so smug," he said. "The only reason you rejected me was because I'm not smooth enough at it, but there'll be others looking for science favors, and they'll get whatever they want from you. From now on, every smile you get will have a hook attached to it."

A few minutes later she got out of the cab and walked up the stairs to her apartment. Nobody was home. She put on her nightgown and went to bed.

After she'd been asleep for an hour, the door to the

apartment flew open. Kimberly and Hal bounced in, followed by four others. "She's here!"

They'd all been drinking. They were standing over her grinning.

"Hey, I saw you in *People* magazine! I loved all those crazy pictures."

"Hal, get these idiots out of here!"

A girl went to the closet and pulled out one of Lisa's dresses. "Can you believe this?" she laughed.

"It's so awful!" another girl agreed.

"Hal! Kimberly! I don't want them in here!"

"Does she have her sheepskin pajamas on?" a guy asked.

"In August?" a girl replied. "Are you crazy?"

"Well, what does she wear in the summer?"

"Get out of here!" Lisa yelled, pulling the sheets up to her chin.

One of them laughed. "Boy, she does have a temper, doesn't she!"

"Hal, get 'em out of here!" she shouted.

"Sure, Hon, just a minute . . ."

She jumped out of bed, grabbed her pillow, and began hitting Hal as hard as she could with it. "Don't you ever call me 'Hon' again!" she yelled at him. Then she ran out of the apartment.

A minute later she sat on the cot in the storeroom, still breathing hard, trying to control her anger. She wiped the perspiration off her face and tried to calm down. She lay down. She could still hear her heart beating. She concentrated on taking deep breaths. In a few minutes she calmed down. She lay there staring at the dark ceiling.

And then she realized she was hearing other people breathe too. Terrified, she sat up and looked around.

There sitting cross-legged on the floor were two men and a woman, all of them staring at the pile of junk that filled the room.

"How long you gotta stare at this stuff before you get feeling good?" one of them asked.

Lisa screamed and ran out.

A minute later she knocked on Mike Anderson's door. It was late at night. He came to the door.

"Can I come in?" she begged.

"Sure." He opened the door. "Here, sit down."

She sat down woodenly.

"What's wrong?"

She broke down crying. He sat by her and waited as the tears tumbled out. A few minutes later she was composed enough to tell him what had happened.

After she finished, he and his roommate left to go run everyone out of the storeroom.

In a few minutes they returned. "They're gone now. You can go back if you want. Be sure and lock the door."

"Thanks."

"Anytime."

"What am I going to do? Everyone's using me. I don't like it."

"Have you thought about transferring to BYU?"

"It'd be the same there."

"Look, here's last year's yearbook. Look it over. See what you think. If you decide to go, we can write my cousin. She works in records there, and she could tell you what you have to do to get enrolled. I'll give you her name and address. You never know, Lisa. It might turn out okay for you there. And it's just about time for fall semester to start."

Lisa sat in the apartment and looked at the BYU yearbook while Mike and his roommate studied. She felt at home with them, comfortable and safe.

Of course, she couldn't go to BYU. She couldn't go anywhere, because it was true what Brent said—she was now a commodity to be marketed. She was a brand-name person. No matter where Lisa Salinger went, people would eventually impose on her privacy.

And then the most ridiculous idea popped into her mind.

The next morning, after Kimberly left for school, Lisa made reservations for a flight to Salt Lake City, then packed two suitcases. She sat in front of her bookshelf trying to decide which books to take but eventually realized she couldn't take any of them, because they all had her name on the inside cover. She needed to leave Lisa Salinger behind when she left the apartment.

She sat in front of her computer and turned it on. It was four years old, ancient now compared to the new models, but it had a certain charm. It was like an old friend. And in a short time it was going to help buy her freedom. She packed the computer in two boxes.

She called a taxi, then sat down to type a note.

Kimberly,

I'm going away for a while. You won't be able to find me, but I'll be all right. Tell people I need time to be by myself.

Lisa

She left the note taped on the refrigerator.

There was a knock on the door. It was the cab driver. She opened the door for him. He picked up her things and headed downstairs.

On her way out, she saw Mike's BYU yearbook on the table. She took it with her to study on the plane.

Six hours later she landed in Utah.

CHAPTER FOUR

I've seen your face some-where before," Mike's cousin Tanya said. They sat in an office cubicle in the administration building at Brigham Young University.

Lisa turned to shield her face. "I look like a lot of people."

"And you're a friend of Mike's?"

"Yes, I met him in New Jersey. I told him I was going west, and he said to be sure and look up his favorite cousin, so here I am."

"What're you doing out here in Utah?"

"Just passing through. How about if we have lunch together? My treat."

"Sounds great, but I've still got half an hour to work before lunch."

"I'll wait. Is that a computer?"

"Well, it's a computer terminal. We use computers so much these days."

"How interesting. Suppose a student sends in an application form, how would the information be processed?"

"I'll show you. First I have to enter the access code."

Lisa's pleasant expression momentarily fell away as she concentrated on memorizing the access code.

An application form flashed on the screen.

"My, my," Lisa said with a deceptively innocent smile.

That afternoon Lisa used her computer and the phone to connect herself with a computer at BYU. She entered the proper access codes, and in a few minutes she was looking at the form for new students.

She felt giddy. She was about to create a person.

Who hasn't wondered what might have happened if, at certain of life's crossroads, they'd taken a different path? For Lisa in high school, the path had been calculus, physics, and chemistry. There was no time for boys, or parties, or being young.

This time it would be different. It had to be. If she kept the same personality, sooner or later she'd be discovered.

LAST NAME:

Her theory had introduced something now called the Salinger Field. She decided to adopt the name Fields.

LAST NAME: FIELDS

FIRST NAME:

Her middle name was Dawn, and she'd always liked the name. She decided to become Dawn Lisa.

FIRST NAME: DAWN

MIDDLE NAME: LISA

DATE OF BIRTH:

She was twenty-two years old. Since she'd never had a chance to enjoy being a teenager, why not try it again? She giggled and entered a date that would make her nineteen years old.

ADDRESS:

Dawn couldn't come from North Dakota too. She picked up a motel map, closed her eyes, and placed a finger on the map. When she opened her eyes, her finger was resting on Grand Island, Nebraska. She called long distance to get the phone number and address of a Burger King drive-in, which she listed as her home address.

HIGH SCHOOL TRANSCRIPT:

Dawn Fields had taken chorus, social studies, typing,

and some business-related courses. No science for Dawn, and only the barest minimum of math. She'd been in drama club, and one year she had been chosen as the homecoming queen.

MAJOR COURSE OF STUDY:

She closed her eyes and pictured Dawn in high school. Dawn loved music. Some said that Dawn always had a song in her heart.

MAJOR COURSE OF STUDY: MUSIC EDUCATION

CHURCH AFFILIATION: (CHECK ONE)

LDS   OTHER

She noticed it was cheaper to be LDS, so she checked that.

Bit by bit she created a Dawn.

The next day she registered at BYU as Dawn Fields. She spent the afternoon at the Provo Public Library reading about the Mormon church and also about Grand Island, Nebraska, in the *Encyclopedia Britannica*. She'd always had great faith in the *Encyclopedia Britannica*, and after she'd studied what it had to say, she felt more than adequately prepared.

That afternoon she took a cab to Robison Hall, where she'd assigned herself from the list of last-minute vacancies provided by the computer.

She found her apartment and knocked.

"It's open!" someone yelled.

She walked in. There was a long hall with bedrooms going off on either side. A girl wearing a robe stuck her head out of the bathroom. "All right, who used up all my shampoo?" She wiped the water off her face with a towel.

Nobody answered.

"C'mon, somebody did."

"You can use mine," another girl called out.

"I can't use yours! I need mine. Mine has flex conditioners. You all know I need flex conditioners. Last night there was just enough for today. So which one of you used it and left an empty bottle for me?"

No response.

"I just got out of the shower. Will one of you go to the store and get me a new bottle?"

Someone turned on a stereo loud enough to cover up her voice.

"All right! This is the last time I leave my shampoo in the bathroom! And you just see if I ever let any of you use anything of mine again. Do you hear me? Now I have to dry myself off, get dressed, walk all the way to the store, buy a shampoo with flex conditioners, which I shouldn't have to buy at all, mind you, if somebody hadn't used it, then come back and shampoo my hair. Isn't anybody listening? Doesn't anybody care about me?"

"I'll go to the store for you," Lisa said from the shadows of the hall.

The girl jumped. "Where did you come from?"

"Grand Island, Nebraska."

"I mean what are you doing here?"

"They said you have a vacancy."

"You gave me such a scare. I didn't see you standing there."

"I don't mind being unnoticed."

"My room's the one with the vacancy, so I guess you'll be rooming with me. My name's Natalie Foster."

"My name is Dawn Fields." It was the first time she'd said it in conversation.

"You're kidding."

Dawn frowned. "How did you know?"

"I just meant I have a sister named Dawn."

"Oh."

"Look, could you really get me some shampoo? I need French Mist Balsam with Flex Conditioners for Normal Hair. Make sure you get the right kind. The bottle is kind of a light green."

"Sure."

"What a pal. I'll shave my legs while you're gone."

As Dawn walked to the store, a girl passed her on the sidewalk. "Hi," the girl said pleasantly.

Dawn looked around to see if the girl was talking to her or somebody else.

The girl passed by.

Twenty steps later Dawn yelled back, "Hello!"

The girl stopped and turned around. "Hello."

"Hello," Dawn called out again.

The girl shrugged and continued on her way.

Strange people, Dawn thought.

She entered the store with its colorful variety of homemade signs advertising weekly specials. While she was there, she decided to buy some things she needed. She got a cart and started down the aisle.

A tall, muscular athlete was standing in the aisle. She passed him.

"Hi," he said.

She decided he was talking to her. "Hi," she said.

"Decisions, decisions," he said, looking at three shelves of cereal.

She decided he meant he was having a hard time picking a brand of cereal. She named her favorite kind of cereal. "Cream of Wheat."

He nodded his head knowingly. "That's so true— Word of Wisdom."

She wondered what that meant.

He placed the Cream of Wheat in his cart. "Wheat for man, corn for the ox," he said, continuing down the aisle.

She paused and tried to figure it out. How few oxen you see these days, she thought to herself.

She was disappointed in the *Encyclopedia Britannica.* They were usually so thorough, and yet in discussing the Mormons they'd never mentioned oxen.

A few minutes later she approached the checkout stand with the shampoo as well as some sprouts and seven containers of yogurt.

A girl stood in line in front of her, talking to her

roommate. ". . . so Alan invited me to the dance on Friday night, but I couldn't go because I had this date set up with Greg, but I really like Alan, and I didn't want to discourage him, so I asked him if we could get together on Saturday, but then I remembered I had a date with Chet that night, but it was okay because Alan was busy then too, so we decided Alan'd come by for me Saturday morning and we'd go water skiing. But the only trouble was I've never gone water skiing before, and so I asked Dave if he'd take me out tomorrow and teach me. So it's working out all right."

Dawn gazed in awe at the girl. She was tall and had long brown hair. Her face was perfect, and yet her beauty seemed so effortless.

A guy walked up to the girl. "Hi, Shauna."

"Dave! We were just talking about you."

"You were, huh? What about?"

"Wouldn't you like to know?" Shauna said.

Dawn leaned forward intently. The conversation wasn't much, but it was spectacular to see how Shauna used her face. It was like a neon sign flashing, "Hey, everybody! Here I am!"

Shauna tilted her head and smiled. Dawn decided it was the teeth and the eyes. What did she do with her eyes to make them so appealing?

Dawn looked at Dave. He lit up being around Shauna.

"Well, I wouldn't be too sure about that," Shauna said, flashing her appealing smile again.

"Oh, you wouldn't, huh?" Dave teased.

Dawn wondered how many calories Shauna used in a day just to keep her face running.

"Well, you'll just have to wait and see," Shauna said, lowering her eyes and then looking up with a sly grin.

"Okay for you," Dave said with a smile.

Dawn leaned forward, entirely engrossed by the interplay of words and body language. She accidentally bumped her cart into Shauna's cart. Shauna turned around, smiled at Dawn, then turned her attention back to Dave.

When Shauna left, it was like someone turned out all the lights in the store.

Dawn advanced to the checkout stand. There on the cover of *Time* was a picture of Lisa Salinger. The caption read "Lisa Salinger—Einstein's Successor?"

Dawn casually picked up a copy of *Seventeen* and placed it over the stack of *Time* magazines.

She was next in line. "Hi there," the man at the checkout counter said. "Trying the Salinger Diet?"

"What?" she mumbled.

"You know that gal who's smarter than Einstein? Well, she lives on yogurt and sprouts. You ought to read about her in *Time* this week. You know, you look a little bit like her."

"I'm not Lisa Salinger."

"Oh sure, I know that—she'd never come here. It's just that you look a little bit like her, the way you do your hair, and your glasses. But they say she's wacko, not like you at all."

"Thank you," she said, grateful to Hal and Kimberly for having created a cartoon character out of Lisa Salinger. "I think I've changed my mind about the yogurt and sprouts." She took it all back and picked up donuts, potato chips, and apples.

Returning to the apartment, she knocked on the bathroom door.

Natalie let her in. "Where have you been?"

"I picked up a few things of my own."

Natalie took the shampoo. "Well, anyway, thanks for going. I'll be out in a few minutes to help you get settled. Our room is the second one on the left."

Dawn unpacked, then went to the kitchen to put her groceries away. Two girls, dressed in warm-up suits, were sitting at the table, talking.

"Are you a new roommate?"

"Yes, I'm Dawn Fields."

"Hey, great. I'm Tami Randall." She was an energetic blonde with her hair in a ponytail.

The other girl's name was Jan Roberts. She had vivid red hair and freckles.

They talked for a few minutes. Tami was a sophomore majoring in drama. She was from Stillwater, Oklahoma. Talking to her was like watching a fireworks display. Her creative mind started on one thought and then suddenly exploded into a hundred peripheral ideas. Dawn wondered if, as a child, she'd been hyperactive. In five minutes, she did three impersonations: Mr. T, Margaret Thatcher, ending up with Joan Rivers, "Can we talk?"

Jan was a sophomore in psychology. She might be overlooked in a crowd, especially in any group containing Tami, but she was good-natured and friendly.

Dawn noticed Jan watching her carefully. She wondered if she was being analyzed the way psychology majors often do to their friends.

In a few minutes the two roommates left to go jogging. Dawn sat at the kitchen table and ate an apple.

A girl came in with a pizza. She had short brown hair and was several pounds overweight.

"Hi, I'm Dawn Fields. I'll be rooming with Natalie."

The girl smiled. "Welcome aboard. I'm Robyn. Want any pizza?"

"No, thanks."

"I can't eat it all, that's for sure. I should've got a small, but they were having a special on family size."

"Sure."

"I've been on a diet. This is the first meal I've had for two days."

"Then you must be hungry."

"A little." She took a large bite.

Dawn left the kitchen. It was the last anyone saw of the pizza.

On her left was an open bedroom. A girl was practic-

ing Spanish to herself. Dawn walked in. The room
looked like a museum, with a bright red Indian blanket
on the wall, as well as several copper plates.

"Hi," Dawn said.

"I'm sorry. I didn't see you. Are you Natalie's new
roommate?"

"Yes. I'm Dawn Fields. I'm from Grand Island, Nebraska."

"I'm Paula Clauson."

"You must like copper," she said.

"Oh, those? I went on a mission to Chile, and they're
just some of the things I picked up while I was down
there."

Dawn imagined a quaint Spanish mission in a small
village where Catholic fathers had a little gift shop and
sold homemade craft items. "You went to a mission and
bought all this? The monks must've been very grateful to
you for giving them the business."

Paula looked at her with a puzzled expression. Finally
she said, "I didn't go *to* a mission, I went *on* a mission."

Dawn paused. "On the roof?"

Paula laughed. "That's very funny."

Dawn smiled. She realized she was giving herself
away. She would have to be more careful from now on.

"It was the happiest eighteen months of my life,"
Paula said.

Dawn couldn't imagine how it could possibly take
eighteen months to buy two blankets and three copper
platters, but she didn't mention it. "Sure," she said, trying to be as vague as possible.

"You should think about going."

"For eighteen months?"

"Of course."

Dawn wondered why she couldn't just order the
souvenirs by mail instead.

She returned to her room and finished unpacking. A
few minutes later Natalie came in wearing a robe.

"What's that?" Natalie asked.

"A computer."

"It looks so educational. Would you mind if I sewed a little cover to put over it when it's not being used?"

"No, go ahead."

"Not that I personally object, mind you. In fact, my fiancé—his name is David—he's a graduate student in chemistry, and he uses computers all the time. He could show you plenty about computers. Do you know what he calls computer programs? He calls them software. Isn't that a hoot? Software. It sounds like a type of clothing, doesn't it?"

"Yes."

"Well, tell me about yourself."

"I'm from Grand Island, Nebraska."

"Really? Do you know Angie Martin?"

Dawn frowned. "No."

"How many high schools are there in Grand Island?"

"Two," she guessed, becoming increasingly annoyed with the *Encyclopedia Britannica* for not having complete information.

"I'm surprised you don't know her."

"Oh sure! Angie—I remember her now."

In time Dawn learned that given any five Mormons drawn at random from anywhere in the world and getting together for the first time, at least three of the five will know somebody in common. She heard many conversations at BYU where the first fifteen minutes were devoted to discussing common friends. "Do you know . . ." is probably the question most often asked at BYU. In time she lived in constant fear of actually meeting someone from Grand Island, Nebraska.

Natalie checked her hair in the mirror. "Well, this'll have to do. David'll be here any minute now. We're getting together with all the graduate students and chemistry department faculty. What do you think I should wear?"

"A dress," Dawn said.

"Right, but which one?" She opened her closet. "As you can see, I'm a Spring," Natalie said.

"So—you think you're a spring?" She pictured springs on cars and buses.

"Yes. What are you?"

She vowed to send a scathing letter to the editors of the *Encyclopedia Britannica.*

"Are you Spring, Summer, Autumn, or Winter?"

Dawn shook her head. "I don't know."

"I'd say you're Autumn, but let me see your wardrobe." She opened Dawn's closet. "Oh, my," she said sadly.

"Is something wrong?"

"I've never seen so much gray in my life."

"It always seemed like such an official color to me."

"If you wear those clothes on campus, nobody'll pay any attention to you."

"I hope you're right."

"You're not fooling me, you know."

"I'm not?"

"You're afraid to let people know how much you long to meet a nice guy and fall in love."

"I do?"

There was a knock at the apartment door.

"That's David. Can you keep him occupied while I finish getting ready?"

David was tall and wore thick horn-rimmed glasses, but the most noteworthy thing was that he smelled like rotten eggs.

"Natalie said she'd be just a minute," Dawn said.

"Typical," David said. "Who're you?"

"I'm Dawn Fields. I'm from Grand Island, Nebraska."

"What are you majoring in?"

"Music education."

He scoffed. "So you came to college to learn to sing songs, huh?"

Dawn forced herself to smile.

"Just kidding. I'm sure it's a good major for a girl. You'll be able to teach your kids nursery songs. Me, I'm a graduate student in chemistry."

"Imagine that," Dawn said with appropriate awe. "Do you know anything about science?"

"Oh no, not me."

"Well, let me tell you something. Life, as we know it, revolves around chemical reactions. Remember that, it's very important. In fact, when I look at you, I don't see a person."

"You don't?"

"Oh, no. What I see is a small biochemical factory. I see stomach acids processing the food you ate. I see hemoglobin picking up oxygen and transporting it throughout your body."

"You mean that life is really just chemistry," Dawn said as naively as she could.

"Very good—you know, there's nothing as challenging as doing research in chemistry. My graduate research project involves a lot of mathematics. Of course, I wouldn't expect you to understand it."

"Oh my no," she gushed. "I wouldn't understand anything as complicated as that. What kind of research are you doing?"

"We're attempting to determine the effect of high pressure on certain chemical reactions."

"By any chance would your research involve sulfur?" she asked, backing away from the smell.

"How'd you guess?"

"Just lucky."

Natalie came out. "Sorry I'm late."

"Typical," David said. They left.

Dawn returned to her room. In a few minutes Robyn came in. "If you want, I'll show you where to store your suitcases."

They walked downstairs. There, in a cage that ran nearly the length of the building, were storage racks for suitcases and skis. And a few feet beyond that was the laundry room with washers and dryers.

"You never saw a storage room before?" Robyn asked.

"What?"

"The way you're staring at all that junk."

"Sorry, I was thinking about something else."

They went upstairs again.

"Want an orange?" Robyn asked. "My dad brought me a case. He's a trucker on a coast-to-coast run. He comes through here about twice a month, and he likes me to eat healthy food. He always says, 'You'll never gain weight eating fruit and vegetables.'"

Dawn took the orange. "Say, when he comes through again, do you suppose he could mail some letters for me? Maybe he could mail 'em from California or wherever he's going. This friend of mine and I have this little game where we post our letters away from where we actually live. Do you ever play that game?"

"No, but I'm sure my dad'll be willing to help."

"Do you want to make a cake or something?" Robyn asked.

"No, thanks."

"It gets so quiet around here at night sometimes."

"I know—isn't it wonderful?" Dawn said.

"What are you going to do tonight?" Robyn asked.

"Either read or hack."

"Hack?"

"That means to program a computer. It's my hobby."

"Sounds better than what I'm going to do, which is to sit around by myself."

"If you want to go out, then go out."

"You mean alone?"

"Of course. Go to a movie or bowling or whatever you want."

"It'd be too obvious."

"What would?"

"That I was alone."

"But you *are* alone."

"I know, but I don't want to advertise it."

"Suit yourself. I'm going to enjoy the quiet."

"I won't bother you. I think I'll bake a cake." She paused. "Do you want any?"

"No, thanks."

"I hate to make it just for myself."

"Then don't make it."

"But I want a cake," she said, wandering off down the hall toward the kitchen.

CHAPTER FIVE

When school began, she was swallowed up in the large introductory classes. She was relieved that except for an occasional "Hi," nobody talked to her at all on the first day.

On Sunday she went to church with girls in her apartment. They met in one of the classrooms on campus. She wore her gray dress and didn't say much.

A girl gave a talk. "Last year my grampa died. He and Gramma lived on a farm, and a few times a year we'd go visit them. When I was a kid, there was this tall tree swing, and I'd sit on it and swing hour after hour, and sometimes Grampa, when he was going from the tool shed to the house, he'd pass by and give me a giant swing, and laugh when I giggled at going so high in the air. I loved to have him hug me, because he always smelled like the outdoors. And one time my favorite horse, Checkers, died, and Grampa took me aside and told me that God lives, and that He'd taken Checkers to another pasture.

"I remember every morning on the farm when we were visiting I'd wake up before my parents were up, and I'd go in the kitchen and there would be Grampa, sitting at the kitchen table, reading the scriptures. He never said much, but he loved God, and now he's with Checkers too, and with God."

Dawn studied the girl's face. There was no doubt about her sincerity.

"... I know that God lives, and that Jesus is the Christ, and that this is the Church of Jesus Christ. In the name of Jesus Christ. Amen."

The girl sat down.

The *Encyclopedia Britannica* had failed to mention a peaceful feeling Dawn experienced during the meeting. After church the feeling left.

She was surprised Sunday night when the six of them knelt for family prayer. Never before in her life had she knelt in prayer with a group, and it seemed peculiar and strange. After the prayer everyone hugged everyone else. They even hugged her.

Lisa Salinger was not affectionate. She felt uncomfortable being hugged, but she didn't say anything about it.

Between classes on Monday she went to the Wilkinson Center. There sitting behind a table were two young men in suits. On the table were several pamphlets about the Church. She began looking at them.

"You're welcome to take some if you want."

"Thanks." She put one of each in her notebook.

She wandered the halls at the Wilkinson Center. One door was marked "The Daily Universe." It was the name of the campus newspaper. It seemed to her an overly optimistic estimate of the paper's coverage.

That night a group of guys from another apartment came over for what they called family home evening. One of them took charge. "Next Saturday our ward's doing baptisms for the dead."

Dawn looked around. Nobody was batting an eye.

"I think it'd be nice if all of us went. What do you say?"

They all nodded their heads.

A series of bizarre pictures passed through Dawn's

mind as she pictured what baptizing the dead might be like.

The guy in charge continued. "One other thing—how many of you have finished your four-generation sheets?"

Dawn pictured an ancient bed sheet passed from generation to generation, from mother to daughter, perhaps on her wedding day.

Paula raised her hand. "Have I ever told you the difficulties in doing the sheets in Chile?"

Dawn pictured the peasants gathered at the side of a river, beating the age-old sheets against the rocks, trying in vain to get them clean.

Strangely enough, though, Paula talked about parish records.

"Oh, one other announcement. We've got meetings coming up in two weeks for anyone in a leadership position."

Dawn wondered how one got into a leadership position. Was it like yoga? Did one practice a few minutes each day getting one's body into a leadership position and chanting "Mmmmmmmmm"?

She decided she'd never recommend the *Encyclopedia Britannica* to anyone ever again.

"Well, Tami and Jan have the lesson tonight. I'll turn the time over to them."

"Well, this being the first of the school year, we thought it'd be good for everyone to introduce themselves. I guess we'll start with me. I'm Tami, and I'm a sophomore from Stillwater, Oklahoma. My hobbies are dancing and drama and sports, especially tennis and jogging. I play the piano, and I like to cook and sew. Let's see, what else? Oh, my goals—my first goal is to graduate. After that, I want to go to Hollywood and act for a while, and then, of course, eventually get married in the temple and settle down and raise a family."

Jan was next. "I'm Jan Roberts, and I'm from Seattle, Washington. I'm majoring in psychology, and so if we ever get stranded out in the wilderness, I'll be the one with no survival skills, but I'll go around asking 'And how are you feeling today?' If everything goes right, I'd eventually like to go into family counseling.

"Tami and I are roommates again this year. I'm sort of the voice of reason for us, and she saves me from having a dull life. I love her a lot, and I'm going to be sorry when we graduate or get married and can't room together anymore. We do a lot of dumb stuff together, like last year we went to *Swamp Thing* with green avocado dip on our face."

The two of them started laughing. "It was her idea!" Tami said, pointing at Jan.

"Nobody'll believe that," Jan countered.

To Dawn it seemed strange for a girl to tell her roommate she loved her. Roommates were to be endured, not loved. Like Kimberly and Lisa.

She realized the only person she'd ever told she loved was her mother, and that was several years ago.

"Natalie, I guess you're next."

Natalie stood up. "I'm Natalie. I guess you all know I'm engaged to David. He isn't here tonight because he had to finish up some important research work. He's getting a master's degree in chemistry, so that tells you how smart he is. He'll get out in April, and then we'll get married in June, and then I don't know where we'll end up. I guess that's about all for me."

"Dawn here is brand new to BYU. Dawn?"

She stood up. "My name is Dawn Fields, and I'm from Grand Island, Nebraska. I'm majoring in music education. Grand Island is situated on the Platte River in central Nebraska. It's the business and shopping center of an agricultural district that produces wheat, corn, and other grains."

One of the guys laughed. "You sound like you memorized that from an encyclopedia."

She blushed. She had memorized it from an encyclopedia.

"What are your hobbies?" Tami asked.

"Hacking."

"Like in hacksaw?" Natalie asked.

"It means writing software for my computer."

"You've got a computer?" a guy asked enthusiastically. "Can I come over sometime and see it?"

"Sure."

"What do you do with a computer?" Robyn asked.

"Well, fun things. I have a program that'll generate all the prime numbers from one to a thousand."

"What's a prime number?" Robyn asked.

Tami broke in. "Let me guess! Is it a really special number? You know, like the year you graduated from high school?"

"No, a prime number is a number exactly divisible by 1 or by itself. For instance, 3 is a prime number, 7 is a prime number, 11 is a prime number."

"What do they use 'em for?" Robyn asked.

"They don't use 'em for anything."

"Then why bother going to all the trouble of finding 'em?"

"Just for fun."

They were looking at her strangely.

Tami broke the spell. "We haven't heard from Paula yet. Paula?"

Paula stood up. "I'm Paula, and I returned from a mission to Chile two months ago. My mission was the best experience of my life. I learned to love the people of Chile so much. I'm majoring in Spanish, and I hope someday I can go back there."

"Robyn, you're next."

Robyn stood up. "I'm Robyn, and I'm majoring in home economics, and my hobbies are reading and sewing." She sat down.

"Gary."

"I'm Gary, and I'm from Nampa, Idaho. I'm majoring in . . ."

Dawn studied Gary as he spoke. He wore clothes

from Penney's or Sears, no designer T-shirts like Hal wore, no chain hanging around his neck. She could almost smell the Idaho sagebrush and see him as a boy helping his dad on the farm or ranch. She felt good being around him—it was more like he was a brother.

The other guys introduced themselves. She was impressed with them, not that they were all that handsome, but they seemed calmer and more mature than any other men their age she'd ever known.

Tami continued with the lesson. "Tonight, I thought we'd work on getting in better shape. We're all going to do aerobic dancing tonight. Jan and I'll lead, so if you'll all stand up and watch us, we'll show you the various steps. Jan, will you start the record?"

Everyone watched Tami and Jan dance to the music. Dawn smiled. She realized Tami had planned it so the guys would watch her dance.

Clever, she thought to herself. I never would've thought of that.

Every day she studied the pamphlets about the Church. It seemed incredible reading about an angel coming to a boy in his bedroom, telling him about gold plates buried in a hill. It all seemed like a version of Dungeons and Dragons.

On Saturday, while her roommates went to the temple to do baptisms for the dead, she pleaded a headache and stayed in her room and did research.

A week later she found a safe way to ask questions about the Church without giving herself away. In another apartment in Robison Hall was a nonmember named Rebecca who'd just started taking the lessons from the missionaries. In Relief Society they asked for volunteers to sit in on the discussions and to do something they called fellowshipping. Lisa learned they just wanted someone to be a friend with Rebecca.

From then on, all she had to do was talk to Rebecca

just before a missionary discussion. "Rebecca, have you ever wondered about this?" When the missionaries came to teach, Rebecca would ask the question. In the process of answering it, the missionaries also taught Dawn about the Church. From then on, she seldom said anything that would indicate she wasn't actually a member.

Three weeks later she was surprised to be invited to Rebecca's baptism. She went just to see what it was like. During the service, she felt that same feeling of calm she'd experienced before. She tried to forget it.

Another Friday night. It was quiet in the dorm. Dawn went to her room and closed the door. She was writing a paper extending her original theory. She had found that the theory could be more elegantly expressed in a six-dimensional formulation using a special mathematical term called a tensor.

While she wrote, she could smell the pleasant aroma of a cake Robyn was baking. She thought about having a piece of it later.

She lost track of time. She loved to work. Her theory now had an existence of its own, apart from her. She had given it birth, but it had moved out into the world, finding both critics and supporters.

Some time later she took a break. When she walked into the kitchen the cake was eaten. She grabbed an apple and returned to her room.

Around midnight she heard the outer door to the apartment open. She crammed her research papers into a notebook and picked up a history textbook.

Natalie burst in the room. "We had a great time at the dance. You should've been there."

"I was fine here," she said.

Natalie sat down next to her. "You need to get out more. All you do is stay in your room."

"I like being in my room."

"Why?"

"I like peace and quiet."

"But nobody's getting to know you."

"That's okay."

"But you're just fading into the walls. Before you get asked out, you've got to be noticed. The competition is tough here, and the girl who doesn't try will surely be overlooked."

"I want to be overlooked," she said.

"Don't just shrug your shoulders and give up. You could be more presentable if you'd just put a little time and effort into it. Let me help you. It'll make life here much more interesting."

"No, thanks."

"You know what David said to me the other night? He said you look like that woman they're saying is the next Einstein. You know, the one who eats eagle's nests and soaks her feet in yogurt. Well anyway, she's suddenly dropped out of sight. Some think the Russians have kidnapped her. David says you look just like her. Have you seen pictures of her in *Time*? She looks absolutely awful. Do you want people saying that about you?"

"Of course not!" she said emphatically.

"Okay then—let me help you."

Dawn nodded her head. "Yes, you're right. I need to change my appearance."

Natalie smiled. "Well, I'm glad you finally agree. We'll get started right away. First of all, do you have any money?"

"I've got plenty."

"That makes it easy. First we'll get you contact lenses, then a whole new wardrobe. No more grays. You're an Autumn, and autumns look good in orange and gold and peach and dark brown. You need warm colors with gold undertones. And your hair style is too short. Your hair is such a beautiful golden brown, so why hide it? Let it grow out. And I bet you don't even use conditioner, do you? You need a shampoo with flex conditioners to make it glow. It's gonna be so much fun to see you blossom. And, Dawn, after we get through, we'll have you meet guys, and then life'll be more fun for you. I'm free Monday after three. Let's go shopping for clothes and makeup and accessories, and you'll be on your way."

Within a week she'd bought contact lenses and gone shopping with Natalie and bought five hundred dollars worth of clothes, makeup, and accessories.

Saturday afternoon when they came home from the beautician, Natalie insisted she go to the dance that night at the Wilkinson Center.

While Natalie fussed over her, Dawn sat in front of her computer and ran programs, not really paying much attention to what was being done to her.

"Okay, I'm done," Natalie finally said. "Now get dressed in this stuff I've laid out on the bed, and then let's take a good look at yourself in the mirror in the bathroom."

While she dressed, she concentrated on what was happening on the computer terminal and not what was happening to her.

She slipped the dress on, put on her shoes, and walked into the bathroom.

Natalie was waiting for her. "Well, what do you think?"

She looked in the mirror. There was a stranger standing there.

"It's not me," she said.

"Of course it's you."

"No, it's the wrong face."

"It's you, Dawn."

She was wearing a pumpkin-colored dress. Natalie was placing a brown silk scarf around her neck, and then put on two small gold earrings. But the most fascinating feature of her face was her eyes. She'd never used eye makeup before, but now with eye shadow and liner, her eyes seemed to take over her face. Every emotion seemed to come more alive. She was like the girl she'd seen in Carson's Market the first day.

"What do you think?" Natalie asked.

"I can't go anywhere looking like this."

"Why not?"

"It's not me."

And yet she was fascinated by her reflection in the mirror.

"C'mon, let's go. I told David we'd meet him at the dance. The whole apartment is going to see you make your debut."

A few minutes later the six of them started for the Wilkinson Center.

"Can I make a suggestion?" Tami asked.

"Okay."

"When you walk, don't look down like you're doing an ant census. And one other thing—can we see a smile?"

She tried to smile.

Tami laughed. "Is that the best you can do?"

"I feel so foolish dressed like this. People will laugh at me."

"Why?"

"Because it's not me."

"They don't know that. Besides, it'll be you as soon as you get used to it."

A few minutes later they arrived at the dance. Dawn was relieved to see that not all the girls were dancing. Some of them stood along the sidelines and watched. Standing on the sidelines was what she wanted most from the evening.

Almost immediately Tami was escorted out on the floor. Natalie left with David to go dance before he had to go back to the lab. Jan was the next to go.

Soon there was just Robyn standing next to her.

"Quit looking down. Look up," Robyn coached. "See that guy over there? He's looking at you. Smile at him."

"No."

"Why not?"

"I don't like this, Robyn. I feel like a roast on sale."

The guy walked over to her. "Want to dance?"

"Not really," she said.

"Sure she does," Robyn said quickly, pushing her toward him.

The guy walked her out onto the floor. The music started. Dawn stood there. He started moving around to the music. Dawn stood like a statue and felt out of place. Her partner had a polite but curious smile on his face.

Robyn came out on the floor. "Dance with him!"

"I don't know how."

"It's easy. You just move around to the music."

"What if he touches me?"

"For crying out loud, Dawn, it's just dancing." Robyn started to dance to the music. The guy looked bewildered dancing with two girls at the same time.

Tami came over. "What's wrong?"

"She won't dance!" Robyn shouted over the music.

"Dawn, watch me. It's easy. Move those feet!"

Now three girls were dancing with the same guy.

The music stopped. The guy saw a chance to escape. "Well, thanks a lot."

Tami started her Mr. T. imitation. "I pity the fool who walks away from this girl in the middle of a dance!"

He stopped in his tracks. The music started again.

"Dance with her!" Tami ordered.

He started toward Dawn to begin dancing.

"What's he going to do?" Dawn asked.

"He's going to dance with you."

"I don't want to dance with him!"

"Try it! It's fun."

He put one arm around her waist and held her other hand. She knew her hands were sweating badly. The roommates left her alone.

"Who are those girls?" he asked.

"My roommates."

"Kind of pushy, aren't they?"

Tami and Robyn were asked to dance. As soon as Dawn was out of their sight, she left her partner and fled the Wilkinson Center.

A few minutes later she walked into the bathroom and looked at herself in the mirror. It was all wrong. She had always felt unattractive, and no matter what they draped around her, she knew it wouldn't make any difference about the way she felt inside about herself.

In the past her mind had accepted her body only because it needed to be carried around from place to place. Now it seemed alien to her.

But still, she had to admit that the woman in the mirror was strangely attractive.

"I wouldn't be too sure about that," she said brightly, imitating the girl in Carson's Market. She smiled at some imaginary guy. "Oh sure, you bet," she laughed. "I'd love to dance with you."

She stopped, suddenly realizing she could carry it off if she wanted to. She could fit in and go on dates and meet guys and master the patter of small talk. But she also realized that for Lisa Salinger, feeling bad about her appearance had fueled the drive to scientific accomplishments. Take that away and she might lose it all.

There was only one thing in her life that really mattered. It was her Grand Unified Field Theory, and whatever followed from it. That was more important than life itself, because it would continue even after she died. She couldn't afford to jeopardize the possibility that she might be able to come up with another equally significant discovery.

She frowned. That attractive woman in the mirror might be her enemy. She would have to be careful these girls didn't make her cheerful.

She vigorously scrubbed off the makeup and, for the first time in Utah, put on her sheepskin jacket over her nightgown and went to bed.

A week passed. No matter how much the girls in the apartment tried to coax her, she quit wearing her contact lenses and went back to her old clothes. She spent her time secretly working on extending her theoretical results.

Sunday in Relief Society, a week later, Dawn was paying very little attention. She was very tired, having worked late the night before.

The girl giving the lesson was from Southern Utah and had a rural accent. Because she seemed so cheerful and friendly, and because she had the habit of ending every statement with "Okay?", Dawn found it easy to discount everything she said.

"I found this really neat scripture in the lesson," the girl drawled, "and I just think we should all listen real good and try to make it a part of our everyday life. Okay? Well, I'll just read it for you.

"'And again, verily I say unto you, he hath given a law unto all things, by which they move in their times and their seasons; and their courses are fixed, even the courses of the heavens and the earth, which comprehend the earth and all the planets. . . . The earth rolls upon her wings, and the sun giveth his light by day, and the moon giveth her light by night, and the stars also give their light, as they roll upon their wings in their glory, in the midst of the power of God.

"'Unto what shall I liken these kingdoms, that ye may understand? Behold, all these are kingdoms, and any man who hath seen any or the least of these hath seen God moving in his majesty and power. . . . Then shall ye know that ye have seen me, that I am, and that I am the true light that is in you, and that you are in me; otherwise ye could not abound.'"

Dawn was suddenly awake. It seemed completely out-of-place, this girl with honey-blonde hair casually tossing off something so remarkable. She had never heard anything approaching it from any of her reading.

"I just think that's so neat," the girl said. "Oh, here's another one that's good too: 'There is no such a thing as immaterial matter. All spirit is matter, but it is more fine or pure, and can only be discerned by purer eyes.' I think it's so special that we have these things to tell us about, you know, the universe and everything. Okay?"

Dawn raised her hand. "What you just read, it might be true."

"Oh, I know it's true," the girl said.

Suddenly Lisa was speaking, and not Dawn. "One of the current theories in physics is the existence of matter more fine than neutrons or protons. They themselves are composed of finer matter, called quarks. Maybe that's what it's referring to when it said finer matter. Or it could have reference to neutrinos. Some scientists feel that neutrinos may make up the major mass contribution to the universe. Tell me, when was that written?"

"Gee, I don't know, a long time ago."

Paula looked it up. "It was in 1843."

Dawn shook her head in amazement. "That's impossible. How could anyone know that in 1843?"

"God knew," the girl giving the lesson said, "and He told a prophet, and the prophet told us, so now we know too."

Although the words were tossed off casually, there was no doubt the girl believed what she was saying.

All at once everything seemed turned upside down. Lisa Salinger was accustomed to truth being wrestled from nature in bits and pieces. Here it seemed to come with no work, and sometimes with little appreciation.

After Relief Society, the girl who'd taught the lesson came up to Dawn. "Thanks for your comments."

"Is it true what you said today?" Dawn asked.

"I know it's true," the girl said with conviction.

There was that same peaceful feeling associated with what the girl said.

It was the first time Dawn ever considered that the Church might possibly become important in her own life.

The next day she nervously stopped for a minute in the lobby of the Eyring Center and watched the Foucault pendulum swing.

She knew she was taking a chance coming to the Physics Department.

On the bulletin board was information about how physics could be a useful major for a girl. There was a copy of the article about Lisa Salinger that had appeared in *Time*.

She fled to the women's rest room and examined her appearance in the mirror. That morning she'd asked Tami and Natalie to help her get ready. They were delighted she was at last taking an interest in herself. By the time they finished, she looked nothing like Lisa Salinger. On the way over she had even practiced talking with a Utah accent.

A girl came in the rest room wearing a spattered lab coat. She started to wash an oily steel rod.

Dawn smiled at the girl. "Are you in physics?"

"Yes, I'm getting a master's degree, that is, if I can ever get the equipment working."

Dawn laughed. "I know, I know. Nothing ever works, does it?"

The girl looked at her strangely. "Are you in physics? I don't remember ever seeing you around here before."

Dawn shook her head. "No, I'm in music education."

"That's probably more practical."

"No, stay in physics. It's a wonderful discipline, and there're so many opportunities in it right now for a woman."

"You mean because of Lisa Salinger?"

"You know about her?"

"Oh, sure. Every girl in physics knows about her. She's our hero, but I'm still not sure I understand her theory."

"It's not that hard if you put it in a six-dimensional tensor notation."

The girl looked at her with a puzzled expression. "I'll remember that." The girl left.

Dawn morosely looked at her reflection in the mirror. More than anything else she wanted to go to the graduate carrels and show the girl the elegance of her theory in tensor notation. But if she did and someone found out who she was, the whole rat race would start up again.

She gave one last practice smile, then continued on her way to the office of Dr. J. K. Merrill, a theoretical physicist like herself.

She knocked on the door. Dr. Merrill answered it. "Yes?"

"I'm Dawn Fields. I talked to you this morning on the phone."

"Oh yes, come in."

The office was cluttered with homework papers and physics journals. He cleared aside a chair for her to sit on.

"You said you had a few questions."

"I know you're busy, so I won't take long."

"What are you majoring in?"

"I'm a sophomore in music education."

"I see. Professor Haines teaches the course in acoustics. Maybe he's the one you need to talk to."

"I'd prefer to talk to you, if I might."

"Okay, go ahead."

She began. "My roommates and I were talking about this the other night—you know how roommates are. Well, we couldn't agree, so I got elected to come and ask you. It's just a little question we have about science and religion."

He smiled politely. "Sure, go ahead. What's your question?"

She made an effort to sound breezy and cheerful. "As I understand it, entropy is a measure of the disorder of a system. Of course, from the Second Law of Thermodynamics we know that isolated systems tend to become more disordered with time. Some, trying to argue for a creation, have argued that the formation of a complex system, such as a human being, could not be brought about by natural selection because it forces a system to go from disorder to a more ordered state. They argue that such a transition would violate the Second

Law of Thermodynamics, and that therefore the earth and its inhabitants were created by God and not by natural evolutionary processes."

Dr. Merrill's mouth dropped open in astonishment. She flashed him her best smile and continued.

"However, it seems to me that those proposing such an argument don't fully understand the Second Law of Thermodynamics. It is perfectly allowable for a system that is not energetically isolated to become more ordered in time. For instance, water freezes into ice, and, of course, water as ice is more ordered than water as a liquid. Therefore, I reject an entropy argument as any kind of proof of there being a God. Furthermore, it seems to me quite possible that worlds could evolve by natural processes, and, in fact, as Carl Sagan has suggested, there could be millions of earths in our galaxy alone that support life. What does the Church say about that?"

He cleared his throat. "You're a sophomore in music education?"

"Yes, sir."

He scratched his head. "I've got to get over there more often. Is that where you learned about entropy?"

She smiled. "Oh no, I have a subscription to *Scientific American*."

He reached across his desk to a bookshelf and pulled down a book, opened it to a certain page, and handed it to her. The heading at the top of the page said "Moses." "Read the part outlined in red there."

She began. "'*And worlds without number have I created; and I also created them for mine own purpose; and by the Son I created them, which is mine Only Begotten. And the first man of all men have I called Adam, which is many. But only an account of this earth, and the inhabitants thereof, give I unto you. For behold, there are many worlds that have passed away by the word of my power. And there are many that now stand, and innumerable are they unto man; but all things are numbered unto me, for they are mine and I know them. . . . The heavens, they are many, and they cannot be numbered unto man; but they are numbered unto me, for they are mine. And as one earth shall pass away, and the heavens thereof even so shall another come; and there is no end to my works, neither to my words.'"*

"I think that answers your question," Dr. Merrill said. "There are many worlds with life. There is a continual process in which worlds come into being, exist, support life, and then pass away."

She frowned. Somehow he had countered her question. "But how do they come into existence? By creation or by evolution?"

Dr. Merrill leaned back and put his hands behind his head. "Let me ask a question. How do you define evolution?"

"Well, a natural process."

"And creation?"

"God just creating something instantly out of nothing by the wave of the hand."

"I see," Dr. Merrill smiled. "There's another possibility. What if God understands natural laws? And what if he uses those laws in organizing matter, which already existed, into an earth like ours? What would that be, creation or evolution?"

It was like a chess game. She smiled politely. "But if the laws of nature existed before God, and if matter also existed beforehand, would that not tend to place God in a secondary role?"

"Not in my mind," Dr. Merrill said.

"Then you don't believe God can create something out of nothing?"

"That's right. Let me have you read something else." He flipped the pages to another section and handed it back to her. She began reading. "*'Man was also in the beginning with God. Intelligence, or the light of truth, was not created or made, neither indeed can be. All truth is independent in that sphere in which God has placed it, to act for itself. . . . The elements are eternal, and spirit and element, inseparably connected, receive a fulness of joy.'*"

"Is this from Joseph Smith too?" she asked.

"Yes."

"Dr. Merrill, you're an educated man. Exactly how do you regard Joseph Smith?"

He smiled. "I regard him as a prophet of God."

She frowned. "How can you blindly accept that he was a prophet of God? Where is the proof?"

He leaned toward her. "The evidence is the Book of Mormon. When I was your age, I had many questions too. I decided to take him at his word—read the Book of Mormon, then pray and ask God if it was true. The same test will work for you too."

As he spoke, that comforting feeling she had experienced before returned.

She shook it off. "I'll read the book, then I'll be back." *To tear it apart,* she thought as she left.

Finally, at the constant badgering of her roommates, she went on her first date. A guy named Greg asked her for a date for Friday to go to a movie called *Cyber Death.* Because of her interest in science fiction, she accepted.

For the next few days, Tami went through the halls doing scenes from *The Glass Menagerie,* rambling on in a Southern accent about "gentlemen callers."

On the day of her date, Dawn reluctantly let the girls get her fixed up. Before the afternoon was over, she felt like a Barbie doll being dressed by a mob of girls.

Finally she looked in the mirror again at the stranger who was taking over her life.

Jan came in and closed the door. "How do you feel?"

"Terrible."

"I know. Everybody does before a blind date. Just talk about his interests and things'll go okay. Do you want to have a prayer before you leave?"

"No," she said flatly.

Finally Greg came, and she was launched on her date.

"It's hard to keep my eyes off you while I'm driving," he said as he drove downtown.

She thought he was joking. "Sure," she laughed.
"I'm serious."
It was odd the way he was looking at her.
"Tell me, Greg, what are you majoring in?"
"Biology. I wish I had a camera to catch your face in dim light. I bet you're terrific near a candle."
Nervously she cleared her throat. "When you graduate, what kind of a job do you want?"
"I want to be a fisheries biologist."
"Tell me, Greg, what did you think of 'Jaws.' Could a shark really become a killer like that?"
"I like your hair too. It shines."
She felt like a new car in a showroom.
He was staring at her. Nobody had ever looked at her like that before. She started to blush. "Greg, what kinds of fish are the most interesting to you?"
"Carp."
"Why carp?"
"In Japan carp is an important fish for food. Carp can eat garbage. Think of all the garbage we've got in America." He pulled up to a parking space. They were half a block from the movie theater, and they could see a line waiting to get into the movie.
"Why don't we sit in the car and talk till the line goes down?" he said.
"Okay."
"Your lips are so inviting," he said.
"You've been spending a lot of time around carp lately, haven't you."
"You're different from all the others."
She frowned. "I don't want to be different. I want to be the same."
He casually put his arm around the top of the seat, which according to Tami was often the first step to a guy putting his arm around a girl.
She backed away. "Let's go see the movie now, okay?"
"I understand. You don't kiss on the first date. I admire that."

"Good," she said with a sigh of relief.

He paused, then asked, "What date do you kiss on?"

"What?" The sound was muffled, because she was holding one hand over her mouth as she spoke.

"Some girls don't kiss on the first date, but they'll kiss on the second or third date. So what date do you kiss on?"

"This is a joke, right? I bet Tami put you up to this." She laughed.

"I love your name. And when you look at me with those eyes, I see uncertainty, wisdom, mystery, and romance."

She moved the rearview mirror and looked at herself. "Where do you see that? All I see is eye shadow, eye liner, and mascara."

"I love the way you smell."

"It's perfume—it comes in bottles. If you bought some and dabbed it on a dead carp, it'd smell like that too."

"And the way your hair shines."

"It's the flex conditioners. Greg, is it asking too much if we could go to the movie now?"

"Why don't you like me? Is it my lisp?"

"What lisp?"

"I don't say some words right."

She paused. "You do lisp a little bit, don't you. Look Greg, I know you're sincere, and in a way I'm sure this is a compliment, but really . . . look, if you really want to make me happy, please take me to *Cyber Death*. If you can't afford it, I'll pay for both tickets."

He was still sulking. "Just forget it."

"Sure thing. Can we go to the movie now?"

Just as she stepped out, while she was still a little off balance, he kissed her on the cheek.

"Greg, cut it out."

"I'm sorry. I don't know what got into me. It's difficult for me to be around you. I like the way you look."

"But it's not me, not really."

He had a pleading look, like a cocker spaniel.

"Greg, quit looking at me like that. Underneath all this gunk, I'm plain and ordinary."

He tried to kiss her again. "No!" she yelled. She hit him in the stomach. He doubled over, gasping for breath. Two couples walked by and looked curiously at them.

"Are you hurt?" she asked.

He was still gasping for breath.

"I guess I'm not used to guys. Sorry. Can you straighten up any?"

"Aaaah," he moaned, still doubled over.

"I bet I hit you in the solar plexis, huh?"

"Aaah."

She looked in the rearview mirror of the car next to them. "You really think I look okay, huh?"

"Aaaah," he groaned, bent over but nodding his head.

She helped him get in the car. He put his head on the steering wheel and fought to get his breath. Finally he spoke. It sounded as if he was about to cry. "I'm so ashamed. I don't know what got into me."

"Hey, forget it. Can we go see the movie now? There's nothing like a little science fiction to take your mind off your worries."

"Will you ever forgive me?" he groaned, holding his head in his hands. "You probably think I go around trying to kiss every girl on the first date. But this is the first time in my life anything like this has ever happened. I'm ashamed."

"It's all right. Now let's go see the movie, okay?"

He wouldn't look at her. "You'll never respect me now."

"That's not true, Greg. I respect you."

"No you don't—not really. I don't blame you. You'll go tell your roommates, and by tomorrow it'll be all over the school. But it's my fault. I've nobody to blame but me."

"I promise I won't tell anyone. Can we go see *Cyber Death* now? Look, there's nobody in the line now."

"It was all my fault. You can't help the way you appeal to men."

"I think cyber stands for cybernetics."

"Every time you see me on campus, you'll think, 'There's that animal.'"

"I promise I won't think that. Can we go see the movie now?"

"What will you think?"

"I'll probably think, 'Oh, look, there's Greg.'"

"You can say that, but I know you'll never respect me again. But what's worse, every time I see you, I'll be thinking, she thinks I'm an animal. Even now I feel so guilty being around you."

"Hey, it's nothing a little *Cyber Death* can't fix."

"What do you mean it's nothing? I showed myself for what I am—a fraud, a guy with no consideration for a girl's feelings, a person with no self-control. It's more than just a little thing."

"Well, it's a little like when a horsefly lands on you—it doesn't hurt, but you're afraid of what might happen."

"You think of me as a horsefly?"

"Greg, don't be so tough on yourself."

"Why not? The damage is done."

"I don't think there's any damage, Greg. So you kissed me. Big deal. It meant absolutely nothing to me. Honest."

"It's not entirely my fault, you know. You looked at me with those eyes—so you're partly to blame too."

She frowned. "They're the only eyes I have. I think maybe the movie's started now, so if we're going to see it . . ."

"I'm so ashamed of myself. I can't be with you anymore. I'm taking you home."

She looked out the back of the car as the sign for *Cyber Death* faded in the distance.

A few minutes later they stood on the steps just outside the dorm. "Sometimes I get so lonely," he said softly, putting his arm around her.

It was the same thing Hal was always saying to Kimberly.

She shoved him away. Unfortunately, someone was leaving the dorm just then. The edge of the door caught Greg in the mouth, cutting his lip and chipping a tooth.

After they'd stopped the bleeding and sent him home, Dawn went into the bathroom, locked the door, and looked at herself in the mirror. She smiled at Dawn's image in the mirror, then went in her bedroom and put on a long white nightgown and slipped into bed. She fell asleep remembering how it had been when she was high school homecoming queen in Nebraska.

"This is not good," Natalie said the next morning at breakfast.

"I'm sorry."

"You can't go around knocking your date's teeth out. Eventually the word's gonna get around."

"I just pushed him a little bit, and he stumbled into the door."

"Was he getting fresh?" Robyn asked.

"Well, he tried to put his arm around me, and he told me he was lonely."

"You beat him up for saying he was lonely?" Tami asked.

"I guess maybe I misunderstood."

"Who's ever going to ask you out once this gets around campus?" Natalie asked.

"It's not important."

"Not important? How can you say that after all the work we've sunk into you? How are you ever going to get married?"

"I don't care about that. Marriage isn't important to me."

"Marriage—not important?"

"There're more girls than guys on this campus. Not all of them can get married while they're here. Why can't I be one of the ones who don't?"

"Are you crazy? Everyone wants to get married."

"What for?"

"God wants people to get married," Natalie said.

Dawn shrugged. "Then let Him worry about it."

"You've got to do your part, and believe me, beating up your dates is not the way to do it." Natalie stormed out of the kitchen.

"Anybody want any more pancakes?" Robyn asked.

"No, thanks."

"Well, there's just a little batter left. Maybe I'll finish it off."

Jan and Tami sat down next to Dawn. "We'll help you. First of all, when you're in the library, where do you study?"

"In a carrel down in the science section."

Tami shook her head. "Why do you study there? It's so quiet."

A few minutes later Robyn sat down to another stack of pancakes.

CHAPTER SIX

It was a Sunday dinner. David and two other guys, boyfriends of Tami and Jan, were eating with them.

"Have you heard this one?" David asked. "If you get a BYU coed and a U of U coed on top of the Marriott Center, which will fall first?"

Nobody said anything.

"The Marriott Center," David chortled. The other guys laughed too.

Robyn put her silverware down and quit eating.

"I've got a million of 'em," David said. "Here's another one . . ."

A few minutes later Robyn excused herself. Dawn scowled at David and left also. She found Robyn in her room, sitting on her bed, her arms folded neatly in her lap. She was staring into space.

"Are you okay?" Dawn asked.

"Oh sure," she said, snapping out of it. "Why do you ask?"

"Robyn, David's a jerk. You realize that, don't you?"

"That isn't a very kind thing to say about your room-mate's fiancé."

"Hey, I'm just getting started. He's also insensitive and pompous."

"'Let us oft speak kind words to each other . . .'"

"Robyn, how about if we take a walk together?"

"Okay."

They walked toward the temple grounds.

"Robyn, if there's anything bothering you, I'm a good listener."

"There's nothing bothering me," Robyn said lightly.

They walked another block. Now they could see the temple better.

"When I was little," Robyn said, "I used to dream about temple marriage. But I don't anymore."

"Why not?"

"Because it's not going to happen," she said, dropping her camouflage of cheerfulness.

"How do you know?"

"I've only had one date in the last two years."

Dawn could see tears in her eyes.

"It's funny in a way," Robyn continued. "The summer before I enrolled here, when I told my friends I was going to the Y, they all kidded me. They said, 'Oh, you'll be married after one semester.' And I'd smile and say no, but secretly I wondered if they were right. But then I got here, and nothing happened. All around me girls were dating, but nobody noticed me. Some mornings now I can't come up with a reason to even brush my hair. What's the use? I can't compete with these girls. Sometimes I get so depressed. Have you ever walked behind a guy on campus and watched him? He scans the crowd, his eyes flitting from one girl to another, like he was in a factory grading potatoes as they go by on a conveyor belt. He's looking for beautiful girls. When he sees one, he'll focus his attention on her until she passes by. Guys spend ninety percent of their time looking at ten percent of the girls. Do you know what it's like to have a guy look at you with absolutely no interest? Like you're a bush or a pillar. On campus it's like I'm invisible. And I'm the one they're making fun of when they tell jokes about fat BYU coeds."

"I hate those jokes," Dawn said angrily. "They're

cruel and demeaning. What right do guys have to criticize? Are their bodies perfect?"

"No."

"So what right have they got to expect ours to be? Hey, who needs a perfect body anyway? Not me. Because if I had one, I'd spend all my time worrying that someday it'd become less than perfect. I'd probably be weighing myself three or four times a day just to make sure I hadn't gained any weight. Is that any way to live? What a trap. And what keeps this going? On TV now we've got twelve- and thirteen-year-old models showing us what we're supposed to look like. Hey, let's face it, Robyn, we're women now, and we can't look twelve years old anymore."

"Still, though, I am overweight," she said.

"You think my friendship depends on what you weigh? You think your future husband's going to weigh you every day and if you gain a pound, he's going to get a divorce? You think happiness means going through life looking ideal? Looking ideal is like putting plastic wrap on a salad. It looks nice, but it's not good for anything. Give me a few scars on a guy, or a few clumps of cellulite on a woman. It all adds character."

"If that's true, guys aren't interested in character."

"Why do we sit by while David, who smells like a sewer, insults us?"

She laughed. "You're a fighter, aren't you."

"Lady, you ain't seen nothing yet. I'm tough as nails."

"Thanks for talking to me. I feel better now."

Dawn broke through her natural reserve and hugged Robyn. "I care about you."

"Thanks, I love you too. Still though, I wish I were thin."

"Fine, go jogging with Tami and Jan. They have a two-mile route around the boys' dorms."

"My thighs'll gross out the guys."

Dawn laughed. "Not after a month they won't. By

then, you'll have strong legs without much fat. Besides, that's what they invented baggy jogging suits for."

She thought about it. "Maybe I will."

"One thing, though, we've got to stop coed jokes. It's not good for girls to be ridiculed like that."

Robyn nodded. "When I was a freshman I knew this girl. She was overweight, like me, but she couldn't stand it, and there's so much of a push to be thin here that she became anorexic. She ended up looking like a prisoner of war. She got so she'd wear only jogging sweats, not to hide the fat, but because she didn't want us to see how thin she was. But no matter how thin she got, she kept thinking of herself as fat. One day climbing some stairs, she fainted and fell all the way to the bottom, and they put her in the hospital. It was her heart. It had been weakened by her compulsive dieting. When she got out, her parents came and took her home, and she's never come back. But nobody cares—not really. Oh sure, we sent her a get-well card, but life here marches on. And there's so many girls here. There's always another to fill the place of the ones who drop by the wayside."

"We'll fight back! We'll unite as women to protest against coed jokes."

"Nobody'll join. Nobody cares. The thin girls tell coed jokes themselves, and the ones like me are too self-conscious to say anything."

"We don't need very many," Dawn said.

The first meeting was held the next week. Four girls attended. They called their group COEDS, which stood for Coeds Outraged by Excessively Derogatory Stories.

"I nominate Dawn Fields as president."

"I can't accept."

"Why not? COEDS was your whole idea."

"I can't be in any position where there might be publicity."

"Why not?"

"I just can't. I'll work behind the scenes, but I can't be in any office."

"Well, okay. I nominate Jan then."

The group's first act was to issue a formal complaint that coed jokes not be printed in the school paper. A week later they met with the dean of students and with Gary Doyle, an assistant editor of the *BYU Daily Universe*. It had been his idea to have a daily column of coed jokes.

"This is an attempt at censorship, plain and simple," Doyle said. "Those jokes are perfectly harmless."

"Well, we don't think it's fair to girls to print those jokes," Jan said.

Doyle smiled. "Hey, if you want, you can come up with jokes about guys. We'll feature one from each side. It'll generate lots of interest."

"We just don't think you should print any jokes that make fun of people," Jan said.

It was clear to Dawn that pleading for fairness would get nowhere with Doyle. She had learned at least something from the lawsuit against Lisa Salinger—people fear being sued.

She broke in. "Listen, Doyle, your newspaper is supported by student funds, and at least half those funds are provided by girls, and yet these jokes are an insult to every girl on campus. If you insist on continuing, we'll take legal action against you."

His mouth dropped. "Who are you?"

She smiled sweetly at him. "Why, my dear, I'm a coed."

He shot back, "What a big mouth you have, coed dear."

The dean of students tried to stop the shoot-out. "I think if we just . . ."

"The better to sue you for ten thousand dollars, my dear," Dawn countered.

He frowned. "You're not overweight, so what's your big gripe about coed jokes?"

She walked over to him. "You're losing your hair, aren't you? I mean it's pretty obvious, isn't it?" She moved aside some carefully placed hair on his head to reveal a bald spot. "I see you try to brush it so the hair covers the bald spot, but we can tell. Girls, look here at Doyle's bald spot. It's kind of funny, isn't it." She laughed and the others reluctantly joined in. "Tell me, Doyle, do you ever worry that nobody'll want to marry you? Just think—another six months and you're gonna have less hair than my grandfather. Doesn't that ever bother you? Girls, let's all laugh again at Doyle's nearly bald head, shall we?"

They laughed.

His face turned bright red. His hand went to his head, and he protectively brushed some hair back over the bald spots.

She sat down. "And that, Doyle, is what's wrong with coed jokes."

The dean of students interrupted their confrontation. "I'm sure we can work this out. We're brothers and sisters in the gospel. There should never be any need for lawsuits. Dawn, I doubt if you're aware of how expensive a lawsuit can be."

"I have twenty thousand dollars in my checking account, and I'm willing to spend it all on a lawsuit. I assume Mr. Doyle has a similar amount he's willing to spend to defend what he believes is his right to insult women on this campus."

Doyle blanched.

"We can't have lawsuits at BYU," the dean of students said.

Dawn pointed her finger at Doyle. "Then get him to quit printing those insulting jokes in the paper, or he's going to be sued. It's very simple. If we get no agreement here today, my attorney will start proceedings tomorrow morning."

The dean turned to Doyle. "I think she's right—those jokes aren't fair. I think you should agree not to publish them anymore."

"All right!" Doyle snapped.

"I'd also like an apology from Doyle in the paper," Dawn said.

"No," he squirmed.

Dawn smiled. "Do you mind if I use your phone? I need to phone my lawyer."

The formal apology appeared in Monday's paper.

But Doyle was not a good loser.

That week an article appeared in *Time* on Lisa Salinger's disappearance. Kimberly and Hal and several of the faculty at Princeton had been interviewed. Kimberly had apparently sold the last of her pictures to *Time*.

The magazine also had a picture of the grade school in Fargo she'd attended, as well as the high school physics classroom. The reporters had talked to her high school friends and teachers. They'd also interviewed her mother. "I hear from her once in a while," she'd said. "She must be doing a lot of traveling, because the letters come from all over the country. I don't know where she is."

Dawn continued to go to the library at least once a week. She would sneak into the area where physics journals were kept and read anything she could find relating to the Salinger Grand Unified Field Theory. In early November she read that two researchers from Europe had reported experimental results that agreed with her predictions.

Also that week she found out that Lisa Salinger had been chosen the winner of the Einstein Prize, presented yearly by Princeton University to a former student. Unfortunately Lisa would not be there to receive the medallion.

However, there was still quite a bit of controversy about her first paper. She read one day that a scientist from Russia had recently criticized her theory. She decided to answer his attack.

Monday night after family home evening she announced she was going to do laundry.

"This late at night?" Natalie asked.

"It'll be all right. I've got some studying to do anyway."

She took her typewriter downstairs and plugged it in, setting it on the table used to fold laundry.

The night rushed by. At four-thirty in the morning she was finished. She put the pages into an envelope. She would have Robyn's father mail it from California next week when he came through town in his truck. She took her clothes from the dryer and then sleepily went upstairs to bed.

"Good morning, sunshine!" Natalie said at seven-thirty, opening the curtains, letting the light stream in.

"Let me sleep," Dawn moaned.

"We can't have you skipping classes now, can we? You'll never amount to anything sleeping. Come on, you old sleepyhead."

The covers were pulled away. Dawn sat up. "What time is it?"

"Time to get up. You're going to look a wreck unless you get up and do your hair and face. Now, come on. Studies are important, you know. You're going to flunk out if you don't start paying more attention to school. Come on, get up. You can sleep after your classes. While you get ready, I need to talk to you. I'm going to help you with your social life. I've already set it up. Next Saturday we're inviting David and his cousin to dinner. Now, quit scowling. It's not going to kill you."

Dawn lay back again and plopped a pillow over her head.

Natalie spent the next few days trying to coach her.

David's cousin was named Cody Wells. Dawn hoped smelling bad didn't run in the family. She was assured that her date was not a chemistry major. He was a civil engineering student who had brought fame to the school by designing, building, and racing a cement canoe against those of other Western universities.

By the time Saturday arrived, Dawn was decked out like a battleship. She was wearing Tami's skirt, Jan's blouse, Robyn's earrings, and a necklace from Chile loaned to her by Paula. At six-thirty there was a knock on the door. Dawn hid in her room and let Natalie get it. As she heard the conversation move from the door into the kitchen, she looked longingly at her computer hidden under its flowered pink cover.

Natalie came in the room. "They're here."

"I know."

"Don't look sad. Be happy. Guys like a girl who's happy."

"I'm happy," she said dully.

"Good—now tell your face. Let's go."

The smell of sulfur dioxide was in the air.

"Hello, David," Dawn said.

"Cody," Natalie said, "this is my roommate, Dawn Fields."

Her eyes opened wide. Cody was sandy-haired, with boyish freckles over a still-deep tan. She thought he was named appropriately because she could imagine him on the jacket of a Louis L'Amour novel.

Dawn smiled. "Hi, Cody."

He smiled back. "Hi."

David smirked. "Dawn here is majoring in . . . what is it, Dawn?"

"Music education," she said.

"Right!" David chortled. "She came to college to play games and sing songs and learn to use a pitchpipe." He chuckled at his own joke.

"Actually," Dawn said evenly, fighting to maintain a pleasant smile, which Natalie stressed was a necessity for the evening, "it's a difficult discipline."

"Oh sure," David chortled. "You have to learn all the verses to the 'Star-Spangled Banner,' right?"

"I'm sure there must be more to it than that," Cody said.

Instantly she liked him for rescuing her from David's superiority complex. She leaned toward him just a little. He smelled good.

"Yes, there is," she said.

"I'd like to know more about it," he said.

He seemed quite at ease with her.

"Oh, there's not much to tell really," she said. "Besides, I'm dying to hear about your cement canoe. Natalie says your canoe beat all the others."

He smiled. "If we're going to be friends, don't call it a cement canoe."

"Why not?"

"Cement is the powdery stuff. If you put any kind of aggregate in, like gravel, then it's called concrete."

Dawn liked the small dimple that appeared like magic when he smiled. And he liked to smile.

He asked what she was doing in her classes. She went to her room and returned with a tuba mouthpiece. She handed it to him.

"Where did you get this?" he asked.

"Brass workshop," she said.

His eyes widened in astonishment. "You made this in a brass workshop?"

"No," she laughed, "a brass instrument workshop. I have to learn to play every instrument, and right now it's the tuba."

She showed him how to hold his lips for the mouthpiece. She blew it, producing the same sound horses make on the trail.

"Dawn, dear, may I talk with you in private please?" Natalie said sweetly.

As they entered their room, Natalie turned sour. "I should think it'd be obvious that noises like that are inappropriate in mixed company. If you could've seen your lips just now! A guy'll never kiss lips he's seen puckered like that." Natalie took the mouthpiece and put it on a table. "Now I know you're new at dating, so let's just leave this here."

They went back. "Dawn, please check the spaghetti while I pour water into the glasses."

They'd rehearsed it all beforehand. It was to make Dawn seem domestic. Checking spaghetti is easy enough to do. One merely sticks a fork into it to see if it's limp. She looked at the spaghetti and said, "Just a couple more minutes." She sat down next to Cody again. He smiled at her and she smiled back.

"I've always wanted to play the tuba," he said.

"Sure you have," she said with a smile.

"No, it's true. Bring it out here, and we'll give it a go."

"Well," she said slowly, looking at Natalie buzzing around the kitchen, "I really shouldn't . . . but . . . I did bring it home this weekend."

"Where is it?"

"In the bathtub."

He laughed. "A tuba in the bathtub? I don't feel so bad now about my battery-powered submarine."

She giggled. "We didn't want you seeing it in my room. Natalie says a girl shouldn't have a tuba in her bedroom."

"Right," he said. "What might I conclude if I happened to see a tuba in a girl's bedroom?"

"I don't know—something horrible, I suppose."

"Probably that she played the tuba. What do you say, let's go get it."

"Okay. I'll get the mouthpiece and you get the tuba."

A minute later they returned with the tuba.

"What's that?" David asked with a scowl.

"It's a tuba," Dawn said.

"I know that. What I meant is, what's it doing here? Aren't there rules against tubas in the dorms?"

Cody and Dawn laughed and sat down next to each other with the tuba on Cody's lap.

Natalie scowled. "Dawn, the spaghetti needs checking again."

Dawn sighed. "The spaghetti is just fine, Natalie."

"I'd like you to check it now," she said tensely.

"Play me a song first," Cody asked.

Dawn got the tuba up to playing position and blew into the instrument. It made a sound like a fog horn.

"Welcome to Mystery Theatre," Cody announced soberly.

"Good grief," Natalie said with a sigh, looking to heaven for help.

"For my first selection I will play 'Mary Had a Little Lamb,'" Dawn said.

It was awful. Cody started snickering and couldn't stop. Natlie started banging pans around loudly. Finally Dawn broke up too.

By then Cody was laughing so hard it was difficult for him to talk. "So you've got this . . . two-ton lamb, and he's going around the countryside . . . maiming wolves . . ."

Dawn roared with laughter. It wasn't delicate and re-fined. It was a gut laugh, coming from deep inside her, past Dawn, past Lisa, into the deep recesses of her mind. It was the way children laugh, open, free, uninhibited, natural, full of joy.

She played a single note, and they both burst out laughing again.

Natalie was not amused. "Dawn, I'd appreciate it if you'd show a little responsibility for this meal and check the spaghetti!"

Suddenly she felt vulnerable. For a frenzied minute, she'd forgotten who she was, whether she was Dawn or Lisa. She put the tuba down and checked the spaghetti. "Just right," she said quietly.

"Now could I have a word with you in private?" Natalie mumbled.

When they got inside their room, Natalie nearly started crying. "Do you honestly think a guy'll ever fall in love with a tuba player?"

"We're having fun."

"Oh sure, he'll let you make a fool of yourself, but

when it comes to taking a girl home to meet his parents, do you think it'll be the girl with the tuba? No sir! Never the girl with the tuba."

"Why not?"

"Are you serious? I should think the answer'd be obvious. Tubas aren't feminine."

Dawn's eyes got big. "You mean there's boy instruments and girl instruments?"

"Go ahead, make fun, but if you ever want to see him again, pay attention. You can play the piano or the violin or clarinet or flute, but the girl who plays the tuba will never go steady. Now, do you care about him or not?"

"Yes, I like him."

"Okay then, you'll just have to do what I tell you. You've pretty much messed things up already, but I think we can undo some of the damage. So listen to me. I'll go in and ask you to drain the spaghetti, and David and I'll leave to borrow some dessert goblets. You say, 'Cody, this pot is so heavy. Can I get you to lift it from the stove and help drain it?' And after he does, you tell him how strong he is. He'll love it."

"Will he wonder how I put the pot on the stove before he came?"

"No, he won't think about that. Guys need to feel strong and masculine now that they've been replaced by electricity."

A few minutes later, with Natalie and David purposely gone, Cody lifted the large pot off the stove and set it on the counter next to the sink.

"You're strong, aren't you," she said. She dumped several pitchers of cold water on the spaghetti to rinse it off, then asked him to tip the pot again so the water would run out.

"How's that look?" he asked.

"Just a little more."

He tipped it too much, causing the spaghetti to suddenly rush out, filling up the kitchen sink, at the same time spilling lukewarm water all over their shoes.

"Are you all right?" he asked. "I hope you didn't get burned."

"I'm fine. I'll get us something else to wear."

She went to her room and changed into a slacks outfit and sneakers. The only thing she could find for him to wear was a pair of gym socks and her old bunny slippers.

He laughed when she brought them in, but put them on anyway.

After they'd scooped most of the spaghetti back into the pot, they noticed the stopper had been left out previously and spaghetti had slid into the drainpipe.

David and Natalie returned with the dessert goblets.

"We're back!" Natalie bubbled, motioning for David to set down the goblets.

"Why are you both looking down the drain?" Natalie asked.

"It's clogged," Cody said.

"Let me take a look," David said, scooting Cody and Dawn out of the way. He looked down the drain, then scowled. "I can see your problem. You got spaghetti in your drain, which means somebody forgot to put the stopper in the drain."

"I *always* put the stopper in the drain," Natalie said, staring at Dawn.

"Well, somebody forgot," David said. "If the stopper had been where it belongs, the drainpipe wouldn't be full of spaghetti now."

Cody tried taking a long knife and reaching down the drain to cut the spaghetti up.

David brushed him aside.

"Let me do it. If you're going to do a job, you might as well do it properly. First we've got to remove the trap down below. Natalie, you'd better watch this, because when we're married, you never know when this'll come in handy."

With a dramatic motion, David opened the cupboard below the sink and pointed. "You see that bend in the pipe there? That's what they call the trap. You see it there, Natalie?"

"Oh, sure!" Natalie bubbled. "There it is. How did you ever know about that? You're so smart. What did you say they call it?"

"The trap," he repeated.

"Why do they call it that?"

"Because it acts as a trap for things that shouldn't be there in the first place if someone had remembered to put in the stopper."

David and Natalie looked at the trap with respect.

"Now what we have to do is remove the trap," David said.

"I've got a pair of pliers in the car," Cody said.

David was shocked. "Pliers? Pliers'd be the absolutely worst thing to use. In plumbing, if you use the wrong tool, you'll wreck your threads. You'd be surprised how many people end up buying new fixtures because they've harmed their threads."

Dawn started giggling at the production David was making out of this. Cody also snickered a couple of times but then tried to be serious again.

David continued. "It's a good thing I carry a complete set of tools in my car. You never know when you'll need 'em. Natalie, here's my keys. Go out to the car, open the trunk, and bring me a pipe wrench."

"I'll get it for you," Cody offered.

"No, you see, Natalie and I are a team. And while she's gone, I'll clear away this junk down below."

When Natalie returned, David, lying on his back with his head in the cupboard, pushed himself out, looked at the wrench, and scowled. "No, dear," he said, "you've brought a crescent wrench. What I need is a pipe wrench. Go out again and bring me a pipe wrench."

Natalie smiled sheepishly.

"It's the biggest wrench in the toolbox."

Natalie didn't move.

"What's wrong?"

"I left the keys in the trunk."

David slid out, sat up, and glared at her. "You did what?"

"Well, I must've set the keys down while I was going through the tool chest and—"

"You locked my keys in the trunk?"

"I'm sorry, dear," she said.

"Sorry isn't going to open the trunk, now is it?"

"I guess not."

He stood up and wiped his hands and glared. "Well, we'll have to get the keys before we do anything else. I've got to go to the lab in an hour and take some measurements, and I need my keys."

"I'm sorry," she said.

"I have to watch you like a hawk all the time, don't I," David said.

Natalie looked as though she was going to cry.

"Now don't start that," David warned. "Just let this be a lesson to you. Next time make sure you have the keys before you close the trunk."

"Yes, dear."

He shrugged his shoulders. "It's water under the bridge now anyway. What we have to do now is remove the back seat, crawl in, and get the keys. We might as well get going. I wish I had my tools."

"I'll lend you my pliers," Cody said with a silly grin.

David nodded and left.

"Are you two going to help us?" Natalie asked.

"What for?" Dawn said. "All we'll do is stand around and watch Mr. Wonderful fix everything."

"The least you can do is show some interest," Natalie said. "It's not his fault the drain was clogged."

Cody agreed. "He might need some help. Besides, I need to get him my tools."

"All right," Dawn said with a shrug. "We'll all go out."

Cody left.

Dawn walked over to her tuba.

"You're not planning to take that outside, are you?" Natalie warned.

"I am."

"You'll never get a husband," Natalie muttered.

"Good."

Cody lent his tools to David and offered to help, but David said he didn't need any help.

A minute later, Dawn burst out of the dorm marching to "Mary Had a Little Lamb."

David gave Natalie a running commentary on his every move as he worked. Every few minutes, Natalie would look up from her respectful attention to David's work and give Dawn a withering stare because she wasn't paying sufficient homage to David. "You don't have the slightest interest in what David's doing for us, do you," she finally said.

Dawn stared back with the same cold glance she was being given. "That's right."

"Just like a woman," David grumbled.

Suddenly Lisa, not Dawn, went on the warpath. She leaned into the car and glared at David, who was on his back unloosening a bolt. "Hey, Mush-for-Brains! Don't you ever play high-and-mighty male around me again! And if I ever hear you put down Natalie again, I'm going to turn the hose on you. Maybe it'll get rid of that wretched body odor of yours."

David jumped out of the car. "I'm not the one who practically ruined the plumbing in there!"

She glared back at him, then stormed off, stopped, and stomped back to Cody, who'd been practicing the tuba. "I don't know how to crochet, knit, garden, make my own clothes, or can food. My life's not going to end if I can't be a wife and mother. I can lift pots of spaghetti without a man's help. I'm not helpless, dependent, or sweet, and I'm certainly not domestic. So that about wraps it up for the entire evening for us, right?" She grabbed the tuba from him and angrily started for the dorm.

"Hold it right there!" Cody called out.

She turned around. "What?" she yelled back.

"You forgot to say that you're impressed with how fast I'm learning the tuba." He smiled at her.

She stopped.

He smiled again.

She smiled back.

Suddenly the mood changed. She faked serious contemplation. "Well, maybe . . . But there're a lot of flash-in-the-pan tuba players. Oh, sure, maybe at first they manage a few good oompah-pahs, but when it comes down to the long haul, they give up. It takes real character to master the tuba."

"Give me a chance," he said.

"Okay," she said softly.

David opened the trunk. "Well, I'm done. Now I need to go to the lab and take another reading. Nat, you want to go with me?"

"Sure."

They left.

Cody grinned at her. "Isn't anybody going to feed me tonight?" he asked.

"Sure. C'mon, let's go inside."

They went in the kitchen. She dished out some spaghetti, and they sat across from each other and ate.

"You've got the most interesting eyes."

She looked away self-consciously.

"But you don't maintain eye contact very long. What's wrong, afraid to look me in the eye?"

"Not at all. I'll prove it. You want to have a staring contest?"

"Sure. The first one to look away loses."

They leaned across the table and stared. He had blue eyes and a wonderful smile, and she felt vulnerable staring into them.

"We forgot to decide the prize for the winner," he said.

"How about an all-expense trip to David's lab and a year's supply of sulfur."

He laughed. "No, I want the prize to be worth something. The winner takes the loser to a dance, and after the dance the loser buys the winner a banana milkshake."

"I don't like banana milkshakes," she said.

"I do, and I'm going to win."

"Oh, yeah?" Without breaking eye contact, she picked up a single strand of spaghetti with her fork, brought it to her lips, and slowly sucked it in, the way she'd done when she was six years old.

He laughed but didn't break eye contact.

Next he slowly reached across the table and pinched her nose. "Beep," he said.

She knew it was juvenile, like kids having lunch together, but she loved it. It had been a long time since she'd allowed herself to be a child.

He reached out and held her hand.

She was blushing. "That's distracting."

"For me too." He let go. "I find you fascinating, and I want to get to know you better, but first I'd better tell you something. There's this girl. Her name is Allison. Right now she's on a mission. We've talked about getting married when she comes back."

She looked away.

"You won," she said quietly. "I'll get us some dessert."

He followed her to the refrigerator. "I was serious about wanting to know you better, that is, if you realize we can't expect too much to come from it except friendship. Allison'll be home in August. So, if you understand . . . well, I do want to be friends."

"Sure, why not?"

She dished him a bowl of ice cream.

"This is a picture, isn't it," Cody said contentedly. "Me here in bunny slippers, you playing songs on the tuba, us sharing a dish of ice cream. Very domestic. I could do this forever."

"That won't be possible," she said. "Next Wednesday I have to turn the tuba in."

"And then what?" he asked.

She smiled. "The trombone."

"One of my favorites. We have to get together for the trombone."

Robyn came into the kitchen. "Anything left to eat?"

"Sure, help yourself."

Dawn introduced Cody.

Robyn ladled out an ample portion of spaghetti and sat down. "Another weekend," she said.

Dawn nodded.

"What does that mean?" Cody asked.

"Sometimes I overeat on weekends," Robyn said.

"Why's that?"

"There's nothing else to do."

"Robyn doesn't date much."

"The truth is, not at all."

"I can change that. Robyn, how about a date?"

Robyn treated it as a joke.

"I'm serious."

"Well, you and Dawn—you know—I don't want to get in the way. Besides, you don't want to go out with me."

"Why not? How about tomorrow night? Isn't there a fireside? I'll take you."

Robyn quit eating. "Dawn, I know you don't want me to go out with him."

"It's okay," Dawn said. "Cody's waiting for a missionary anyway, so we're going to be just friends. Go ahead."

"Okay, I will. Thanks."

Sunday night while Cody was out with Robyn, Dawn spent time reading the Book of Mormon.

The next day after classes, Cody walked her back to the dorm. While he waited in the lobby, she went in to change clothes. He was going to take her to one of the civil engineering labs and show her how to make concrete.

She saw Paula in bed and went in to investigate. "What's wrong?"

"I'm sick. I want a priesthood blessing. Is Cody here?"

"Yes."

"Ask him."

She went out to the lobby. "Paula's sick. She says she wants a priesthood blessing."

"Sure. I'll get my roommate and be right back."

A few minutes later, with Paula in a robe sitting on a chair in the kitchen, Cody and his roommate solemnly placed their hands on her head. Cody sealed the anointing. "By the power of the priesthood, we seal this anointing, and give you a priesthood blessing . . ."

Dawn looked at Cody. His eyes were closed, his hands gently resting on Paula's head, his words gentle and kind and calm. There was that calm feeling again in her heart.

Tears crept down her face. She had never known a man could be tender, compassionate, and caring.

A few minutes later they were in the civil engineering lab up to their elbows in concrete.

"Thanks for taking Robyn out Sunday. It really helped her."

"Glad to do it. She's a nice girl."

"You care about people, don't you."

"I guess so."

"I haven't known guys who cared about anything but themselves. I find it very—well—attractive."

And then he did something else very appealing to her—he blushed. "Thank you."

That night she dreamed about him.

The next day after classes, because it was a warm day for November, they hauled last year's concrete canoe out to Utah Lake. She brought along her trombone.

He paddled a ways out. She put the trombone together and played for him.

"How romantic," he said when she finished. "A girl playing love songs for me."

"'Twinkle, twinkle, little star'—not much of a love song."

"But it was played with deep feeling," he said.

"Maybe." She smiled.

This is flirting, she thought, *and I love it.*

"I like you," he said.

"Is it me, or my access to musical instruments?" she teased.

"It's you, Dawn," he said, suddenly serious.

She looked away.

"There you go again. Are you hiding something?"

"Why do you ask?"

"Your eyes. Is there someone else in your life?"

She paused. "I guess there is."

"That explains it. I guess the most we can hope for, for both of us, is friendship."

"I guess so. The other person in my life is very demanding of my allegiance." She didn't tell him the other person in her life was Lisa Salinger.

But even as she said it, she realized, almost sadly, that she was falling in love with him.

"You came back," Dr. Merrill said as she walked into his office. "Just a minute." He picked up the phone. "Send Donna Satter to my office, will you please?" He hung up and turned his full attention on Dawn. "Have you read the Book of Mormon?"

"Yes."

"And have you prayed and asked God if it's true?"

"No, I haven't."

"Why not?"

She paused; then with half a smile she said, "I'm afraid I might get an answer."

"What's the worst thing that could happen if you found out the Church is true?"

"If I was sure it was true, I'd have to get baptized."

"You're not a member then?"

"No, sir."

"And it would be so terrible to be baptized?"

"So far I've only had one major goal in my life."

"And what's that?"

"To achieve excellence. If I joined the Church, then there'd be two goals. I like the way things are now. And that's why I haven't asked the question."

"You're afraid of the answer?"

"I guess I am."

"You're extremely intelligent, aren't you."

"Yes, sir."

"That's a gift of God too, you know. Don't pit one gift of God in your life against another. He knows you by name, and He's pleased with what you've accomplished in science."

She tensed up. "Science? What do you mean? I'm a music education major."

"Something interesting happened the first day you visited me. One of our graduate students told me she'd talked to a girl that same day. This mysterious stranger told her that the Grand Unified Field Theory is best understood in six-dimensional tensor notation. Later my graduate student asked me what that meant. I told her I didn't know."

The girl Dawn had talked to suddenly appeared in the hall outside his office.

"Donna, is this the girl you were telling me about?"

"Yes, it is."

"Thanks, Donna."

The girl left. Dr. Merrill continued. "I didn't think anything more about it until a few days ago, when I received my latest copy of *Physical Review Letters*. It has a paper by Lisa Salinger outlining her theory in a new six-dimensional tensor notation. The question is, how did a music education major know something about Salinger's theory that hadn't even been published yet? You want to

know what I think? I think you're Lisa Salinger. I admire
you a great deal. Let me be the first to welcome you to
BYU."

She turned crimson.

"Don't worry, I won't tell anyone you're on campus.
And Donna doesn't know who you are. Your secret is still
safe."

Dawn nodded and quickly left.

CHAPTER SEVEN

After finals in December, she told everyone she was going home for Christmas. But instead of going home, she flew to California and spent three weeks at UCLA writing another paper. She phoned her mother Christmas morning.

"Some reporters have been here this week asking about you. What shall I tell them?"

"Tell them I called from California."

Classes began the first week in January. She went on a date with Cody on Friday night. He told her that while he was home for the holidays, he'd spent a few hours talking to Allison's parents about her mission. Dawn listened, a polite smile frozen on her lips.

Early Saturday morning the phone rang. Tami answered it and knocked on her bedroom door. "Dawn, it's for you. It's a guy."

She padded out in her slippers and answered it.

It was Cody. "I'll be by in half an hour. Wear warm clothes—long underwear, if you've got it. Don't bother to eat breakfast. Any questions?"

"Just one," she said. "Who is this?"

"Very funny," he said, hanging up.

She had planned to spend the day in the library reading physics journals, but suddenly that didn't seem very important.

Half an hour later he picked her up.

"You're supposed to ask for a date well in advance," she teased.

"You look beautiful in the morning."

She softened. "I just don't want to give you the impression that all you have to do is whistle and I'll come running."

"I didn't whistle. I phoned."

"Okay, it's all right then," she said with a smile.

At a stop light, they were lost to the world looking at each other.

"Where are we going anyway?" she asked.

"I'm not sure. I'm really getting confused," he said.

"Roadwise, I mean."

"You'll see."

A few miles into Provo Canyon, he made a turn and started up a steep road heading into the mountains. A few minutes later they pulled into a campground. He opened his trunk and pulled out a Coleman stove, a sack of groceries, and a large frying pan.

"You make the flapjacks, and I'll build us a fire to keep warm."

He scooted the snow off the picnic bench and put down a blanket for them to sit on.

"I love it out here, don't you?" he asked.

"Yes, it's really nice," she said enthusiastically, only partially deceiving him. It was nice, but her feet were cold.

"I can't stand to be locked up inside. I have to be outdoors. That's why I got into civil engineering. Are you warm enough?"

"I'm fine."

She was grateful that he made a blazing fire, using wood from the trunk of his car. She mixed up the pancake mix while he laid a tablecloth on the table.

She cooked a pound of link sausage first, then turned out pancakes until they both were full.

He brought out two sets of snowshoes from the car.

"Let's go." They trudged through the forest. The snow was four feet deep in places. Nobody else had been there all winter, so every step they made on snowshoes was the first mark.

A few minutes later they stood on top of a hill looking down on a snowy world below them.

"It's beautiful," she said.

"I'm glad you like it. I wanted to share it with you. These woods, and the snow, even the cold, even the wind when it cuts through you, all of it, all of nature—there's nothing phony about it."

She recited the poem "Stopping by Woods on a Snowy Evening" by Robert Frost.

"When did you learn that?"

"High school."

"I wish I'd known you then."

"Why?" she asked cautiously.

"Just to have a friend. But I probably would've had to stand in line. I bet you had lots of boyfriends in high school, didn't you."

"Not really."

"I don't believe that. Dawn, you're . . . my best friend."

"Oh."

"I don't know how to say this, or even what I should say, but these past few weeks—I've never felt so happy being around a girl. Dawn, I like you a lot," he said, softly touching her cheek.

"This is dumb, you know," she said, trying not to be captured by the magic.

"You mean being up here on snowshoes?"

"No, that part's all right. It's just that I keep thinking about Allison. Tell me again what a wonderful person she is, and when she gets off her mission."

She'd spoiled it.

"We'd better get back down," he said soberly.

They walked to the car and took off their snowshoes. Before getting into the car, she picked up a pile of snow and tossed it playfully in his face. He yelled as the snow hit him and then started chasing her. She ran away laughing. When he caught her, he gently pushed her into a snowdrift.

Suddenly the snow wasn't cold anymore. It was a wonderful playground. When he reached over to pull her out, she pushed him down and threw snow in his face.

He chased her. They both were laughing so hard they couldn't finish their sentences, and the words came out between gulps of laughter.

When he caught her, he reached down and scooped up a pile of snow. He was going to throw it, but he made the mistake of gazing into her eyes. He dropped the snow, and they embraced and kissed.

He had his arm around her waist as they walked back to the car.

"When I saw you come busting out of the dorm playing the tuba, I said to myself, there's the girl for me, someone who's happy just being herself—somebody who doesn't go around putting up a phony image."

"Oh," she said, turning away so he wouldn't see the guilt in her eyes.

After that, they spent most of their free time together. Because he was her first romance, she deeply meant every one of the goodnight kisses they shared.

Her only frustration was how he could continue seeing her without writing Allison and breaking up with her. Somehow he was able to compartmentalize Allison and Dawn into separate places in his mind. Perhaps, she thought one day, it was the same way she compartmentalized Dawn and Lisa. She wasn't exactly sure how Lisa felt about Cody.

As time passed, the tension she experienced also grew.

The end of March came like a lion. Dawn, Robyn, Paula, and Cody sat on the edge of the indoor swimming pool on campus, dangling their feet in the water. It was Cody's idea to invite Robyn and Paula. They'd just finished a game of water basketball, the three girls against Cody.

Paula told a story about her mission.

"Is there life after a mission?" Cody teased when she finished.

Paula smiled. "You're right—that's all I ever talk about. It's just that everything else seems so unimportant."

"Sure, a mission's important. But once it's over, a person needs to start thinking about other goals in life."

Dawn smoldered inside. At first it had seemed all right for her and Cody to do things with her roommates, but lately she resented their hanging around.

"Nobody's noticed it, but I lost two pounds last week," Robyn said.

"Way to go, Robyn!" Cody encouraged.

"I've been jogging with Tami. She's like honey around flies when we get around the boys' dorms. They always stop and talk to us. I've met at least a dozen really neat guys. It's so much fun to talk to 'em. I love it. No more late-night cakes for me."

"You can do anything you want to," Cody said.

"You started it all by asking me out."

"Hey, we had fun that night, didn't we."

Dawn dove into the water and swam as fast as she could to the other side. *I'm jealous,* she thought. *How stupid. It's impossible for me to fall in love here. I'm not one of them and I never will be.*

She stopped at the other end and glared at them.

Cody pushed off and swam toward her. His strong arms carried him easily through the water.

She didn't want to talk to him.

When he reached the other end, he looked around and saw that she'd moved. He headed toward her. She swam away, but he pursued. A short time later he came up behind her and grabbed her legs. She quit swimming. They treaded water.

"Hi," he said. "Want to play tag? You, me, Robyn, and Paula."

"I'm tired of playing games."

"Let's touch the bottom with our feet, okay?" He put his arms on her waist. "One . . . two . . . three!" They descended. She opened her eyes underwater. He was smiling at her, and bubbles were streaming from his mouth. They touched bottom, and he kissed her. She was furious with him and shot to the top for air, then swam away.

He thought it was a game, and he chased and caught her again, laughing and playful. "Let's do that again!"

"Get away from me! I'm not your water playmate!" she shouted. "Why don't you wait for Allison to come back, and then you can maul her underwater all you want? You've strung me along when you know you're never going to get serious. But it's my emotions you're playing with. Well, I've had it!"

She stopped and looked around. Everyone in the pool was staring at her. She stormed into the women's dressing area.

In the shower, her tears mingled with the water streaming down her face. She didn't want to share him with anyone, not with Paula, not with Robyn, and especially not with Allison.

He drove them all back to the dorm and parked the car in the parking lot. Robyn and Paula, feeling the tension in the car, quickly escaped.

Dawn started to get out too.

"Wait," he said, "we need to talk. What's wrong?"

"When does Allison get off her mission?"

He sighed. "The first part of August."

"Will you be on campus then?"

"No, I'll be working on a highway crew for the summer. What about you?"

"I'm going to summer school."

"How about if I come up and see you on the weekends."

"You mean before Allison gets home?"

"Yes."

"And what about after?"

"We'll have to wait and see." He cleared his throat. "Dawn, let me explain. You caught me off balance. I didn't expect—" he paused, "we'd become so close."

"You just needed someone to fill in for her. I mean, with her gone, you were lonely, weren't you."

"Yes."

"Okay, now it's my turn to be lonely. Cody, I don't want to ever see you again." She made it to her room before she broke down. She was glad he hadn't seen her cry.

"It was the tuba," Natalie said quietly. "I could've told you."

"I hate him," she said.

"Next time do what I say, okay? I know about these things."

"There won't be a next time."

"There's always a next time."

The semester ended in April. Cody went away for the summer. Dawn took summer classes.

To help time pass, she got a job at the Wilkinson Center snack bar.

In June Natalie and David were married in the temple. Dawn attended the reception. She was relieved that at least for that occasion David smelled like a normal person.

That summer she read the Bible, the Doctrine and Covenants, the Pearl of Great Price, the Book of Mormon, *A Marvelous Work and a Wonder, Articles of Faith,* and *Jesus the Christ.* She found on campus a scholar in ancient

languages. She took a class from him. He was incredibly
intelligent and yet possessed a strong testimony. By the
time the class was over, she had enough intellectual confidence in the teachings of the Church to allow herself to
fast and pray for an answer.

The answer came with a renewal of those same feelings of peace and calm she'd felt from the very first time
she attended a sacrament meeting.

She decided to get baptized. The only problem was
that her roommates already thought she was a member.
To admit she hadn't been a member before might
jeopardize her existence as Dawn Fields. She decided to
get baptized off campus.

The next Sunday she drove a rented car to Brigham
City, some ninety miles north of Provo, and went to
church. During sacrament meeting she looked around
the congregation to make sure she didn't know anyone
there. After the service, she saw two missionaries. She
walked up to them and said, "I want to be baptized."

They both grinned. "How much do you know about
the Church?"

"I know quite a bit." She told them the books she'd
read during the summer.

"Where do you live?"

"Just a couple of blocks from here," she lied. "I just
moved in."

"Give us the address, and we'll come and give you the
lessons."

"I don't want the lessons. I want to be baptized."

"We're supposed to give you the lessons."

"Give them to me here at church then. Today, if possible. I'm living with my father, and he doesn't want to
have anything to do with the Church."

Ten minutes later they started on the lessons, but it
soon became apparent she knew a great deal about the
Church. "Okay, when would you like to be baptized?"

"Today would be good for me."

"Is it okay if we interview you first to make sure you're living the right way?"

"Sure. Go ahead."

"I need to ask a few questions. First of all, do you believe in God and in Jesus Christ?"

"Yes."

"Do you understand that when you're baptized, you enter into a covenant with God to do his will? You'll be taking upon you the name of Jesus Christ. Are you willing to do that?"

"Yes."

"Do you believe that Joseph Smith was a prophet of God?"

"Yes, I do."

"Do you sustain the president of The Church of Jesus Christ of Latter-day Saints as a prophet, seer, and revelator?"

"Yes."

"We've been told by revelation that certain things aren't good for our bodies, things such as smoking, or using alcoholic beverages, or drinking coffee or tea. Do you live that principle?"

"Yes."

"We've been asked by the Lord to share ten percent of our income with him by paying tithing. Are you willing to be obedient to that commandment?"

"Yes."

"God has reserved sex for marriage. Are you living within those guidelines?"

"Yes, I'm morally clean."

"God expects us to be completely honest with our fellowmen. I assume you always tell the truth."

Suddenly her shoulders slumped and her confidence vanished.

"Is anything wrong?"

She realized she couldn't go through with it. Dawn Fields was a fraud. She didn't really exist. What good

would it do to enter a covenant with God under a false
identity?

She stood up, tears filling her eyes. "I'm sorry for
troubling you, but I can't be baptized."

She drove back to BYU.

Eventually fall semester began. With Natalie married, Dawn roomed with Robyn. Over the summer she'd
firmed her body by eating regular meals, cutting out
sweets late at night, and regular exercise. Tami and Jan
were still together. Paula's new roommate was a
freshman from California named Kelly O'Dougherty.
She was very tan. They guessed that her family was rich,
because her wardrobe came UPS in five shipments.

Dawn now felt comfortable in the clothes and
makeup Natalie had suggested. Her hair had grown long
enough to require putting it up every day. She'd even
dated a little over the summer, but nothing serious.

Seeing her on campus, even with a photograph of
Lisa Salinger in your hand, one would never be able to
pick her out of the sea of thousands of other well-
groomed coed faces.

The first night the roommates were together again
they stayed up late talking and snacking. Tami talked
them all into going to an apartment of guys in their ward
they'd known the year before and serenading them with
songs from *Sesame Street*. Afterwards they were invited in
to play charades.

Back in the dorm again, they moved their mattresses
in the large kitchen so they could be together all night.

Sometime during that night, with Tami and Paula
doing ad lib TV commercials, Robyn doing aerobic exercises in the hall, and Jan quietly analyzing everyone else,
Dawn looked around and realized she loved her roommates.

At eleven o'clock they ordered two pizzas to be delivered.

When they came, Robyn had a small piece of pizza and an orange.

After school started, Cody didn't phone. Once Dawn saw a girl walking with him. It was Allison. She was very pretty.

Dawn continued to work at the snack bar in the Wilkinson Center. Once a day she saw Doyle in the supper line. He was the editor of the *Daily Universe* that year. "Sometime this fall we want to do an article about you. Don't worry, I won't write it. I'll have a reporter come and talk to you."

"Don't bother. I lead a very boring life."

"It wasn't my idea. The girls on the staff say they'll quit unless we do a story about you."

After that, someone named Cindy Dyer began leaving phone messages, but Dawn never answered them.

She was taking a music class called Essentials in Conducting. Once a week students got a chance to conduct the orchestra for a few minutes. Because her last name was Fields, her chance came early on in the semester. On that day she was second in line.

The first conductor, a girl named Pam, started the orchestra. They made a mistake, and she stopped them. She smiled. "Now you're doing real good, okay? But I think there might have been just a tiny little mistake back there at G. Let's play it again at G, okay?"

They played it again and continued to make the same mistake.

She stopped them again. "Gee, I hope you don't mind me stopping you all the time, but it still doesn't sound right to me. I know you can do it better, okay? So let's all work really hard this time and see if we can do it even better. Okay?"

"Time," the teacher called. "Fields, you're next."

She took her place in front of the orchestra. "Take it at G," she said crisply.

They murdered it again.

She blew up. "What are you people doing?" Someone laughed. She glared at the offender. He quit. She pointed at the first-chair French-horn player. "What's your name?"

"Alan."

"Alan what?"

"Parker."

"Parker, play it at G."

He played it badly.

She pointed to the second-chair person. "What's your name?"

"Williamson."

"Play it at G."

He played it right.

"Parker, you now play second chair. Change places with Williamson. He'll play first chair."

Parker smirked. "You can't do that."

She slammed the baton against the music stand. "For the next four minutes and thirty seconds I'm the conductor of this orchestra. And while I am, I'll do anything I please. Now move!"

Parker looked to the instructor for a reprieve. Finding none, he grumpily moved to second chair.

They played it again at G. This time it was right.

There was a critique afterwards.

They loved Pam.

They hated her.

She fumed about it all that night. Finally she complained to Jan. "If I'm sweet and docile, then I'm seen as feminine but ineffective. But if I assert myself and try to be professional, then I'm seen as domineering but not feminine. I can't win. All I want is to be feminine and professional. Why does that seem to be impossible around here?"

"Would you like to know a few things I've noticed about you?" Jan said.

She tensed up. "Why not? That's the price we pay for having a psychology major rooming with us."

"Most of the time you're mild and pleasant, but at other times, something sets you off, and you become almost militant. I noticed it first when you talked to Doyle about coed jokes. Is there any reason why you'd have a split personality?"

She tried to make light of it. "C'mon Jan, it's me. Don't try analyzing your roommates. I mean, isn't everyone a little crazy? Sure I get mad at times, but that's all there is to it."

Jan looked at her, smiled, and backed down. "Sure, I must've been mistaken."

In October Cody came to see her at the snack bar while she was working.

"I've been thinking about you."

Keep it breezy and light, she told herself. "They say if your ears are itching, that means someone's thinking about you. My ears were itching yesterday. Were you thinking about me at six-thirty last night?"

"I can't remember the exact time," he said.

"Of course, it may just be my shampoo. I think I'm allergic to flex conditioners."

"I'm sorry I didn't come by sooner."

"Oh, my, don't apologize. I've met so many nice guys since you dumped me."

"You're the one who refused to see me anymore."

"And how is good old Allison?" she asked with a plastic smile covering the tension she felt.

"Fine."

"I bet you're both real busy what with wedding plans and such." Another pleasant smile.

"Not exactly."

"Why not?"

"I can't get you out of my mind. Allison considers that a real drawback in our relationship. She told me to decide once and for all."

She noticed that her voice was getting shrill. "I'll make it easy for Allison. Forget me. I'm not real. I belong in a magic bottle. I lived there hundreds of years until some poor soul opened the top. I'm somebody else, so don't love me." Another smile.

Now he'll leave me again, she thought miserably, *and go back to Allison.*

"Excuse me," a girl said, reaching past Cody for a tossed salad.

"You're blocking my customers," Dawn scolded.

"I'm a customer too, you know."

"You're only a customer if you buy something."

"Okay, I'll take a banana." He reached for one on the mechanical lazy Susan.

"Sure—it figures," she said bitterly, realizing she'd just lost "breezy and light."

"What does?" he asked.

"That you'd want a banana."

"What do you mean by that?"

"Go ahead, take the banana, get your satisfaction out of it, then just toss aside the peel. That's what you do, isn't it? That's what all the guys around here do."

He grinned. "You want me to eat the banana peel."

"Do whatever you want. Do what every guy on this campus does."

"Which is?"

"Date a girl until her expectations are up, let her knock herself out baking bread and inviting him to supper, and then dump her for somebody else. You think we like making bread?" She couldn't help sounding bitter.

"When did you ever bake me bread?"

"Plenty of times. I just never gave any of it to you."

"Why not?"

"It tasted awful."

He laughed. "If I wanted bread, I'd go to a bakery."

"Excuse me," a guy said, reaching for a chef's salad.

"You're in the way again," she said. "Let my customers get the food they want."

"Miss, I'd like a Jell-O, please," Cody called out.

"There's none on the counter."

"Okay—where have you hidden it?"

"You want me to get you some, is that it?"

"That's what you're paid to do, isn't it?"

She left and in a short time returned with his Jell-O. "Here."

"Thanks."

"Don't mention it. Like you said, I'm paid to do it."

"I'd like to start going out with you again," he said.

"What for?"

"I can't get you out of my mind."

"Forget me," she said. She bumped a chef's salad with her elbow, and it fell on the floor. "Now look at what you made me do."

She knelt down and quickly scooped the salad back onto the plate. He leaned over the counter to watch her. "You're wound tighter than a drum. What's wrong?"

"It's hard for me to be around you," she admitted. When she stood up, she hit her head on the counter.

"Are you okay?"

"I'm fine," she answered tensely, rubbing her head.

"Why is it hard to be around me?"

"I'd rather not say."

"If you don't want to say it, maybe you'd be willing to write it in whipped cream on top of my Jell-O."

"Very funny."

"I thought so."

"I'm sure you did."

"Meaning what?"

"It fits your level of maturity," she said, still rubbing her head.

"And you're way above that, right?"

"Listen, I'm smarter than you've ever given me credit

for. If you like me, then you have to like my mind too. It's a package deal."

"I like your mind. I enjoy the challenge of talking to you. You think I'd stand here and watch my Jell-O warm up with just anyone?"

"Why can't you ever frown once in a while? To you everything's a game. The whole trouble with our relationship was that we never talked about substantative issues."

"Substantative issues," he mocked. "Like what?"

"Like acid rain. Trees are dying every day, but do you care? No, of course not."

"I'm sorry they're dying, but what can I do about it?"

A girl going through the food line stopped to watch them.

"Besides, what have you ever done for a tree?" he asked.

"Excuse me, I've got to work."

She concentrated on putting out trays of desserts. A minute later he stood next to her, helping her work.

"This is a restricted area. It's just for Food Service employees."

"They just hired me. You're supposed to train me. Go ahead and work. I'll pick it up as we go along. We were talking about trees."

She turned to glare at him. "We weren't talking about trees. We were talking about our past relationship. It was superficial, just as this conversation is superficial."

He saw a white apron and put it on. "Hey, don't knock this. I'm enjoying every minute. The thing I missed most about you was the challenge of trying to figure you out. And we had good times together. Remember the time we cooked our breakfast in the snow."

She dropped a dish of butterscotch pudding on her shoe.

"Don't worry," he said. "I'll clean it up."

"I never drop things," she tried to explain. "It's just because you're here."

"It's all right. I understand."

He took a towel and wiped it up. "There, I got most of it."

"You liked the time we spent together?" she asked hopefully.

"Best time I ever had."

"But it was all superficial. We'd go to a movie or a dance, maybe have a treat, then pull up to the dorm, and talk. And maybe we'd kiss. Is that all there is to a meaningful relationship? I'm more than just a pretty face."

He followed her into the food preparation area, where she picked up a tray of chef's salads from a large refrigerator.

"Are you saying that nobody fully appreciates your splendor?"

He carried the tray to the food counter for her. They put the salads on the lazy Susan. "I'm saying there's a part of me that nobody here at BYU knows."

"Okay, show me."

She paused. "I can't show you here."

He looked at her strangely. "Why not?"

"It's not something I show, it's something I explain."

"Okay, after you get off work, tell me." He started on his Jell-O.

"I'd better warn you, it's going to be a serious discussion."

"Terrific."

"It won't be easy, but I'll tell you everything."

"Okay."

"But you've got to promise not to tell anyone."

"I won't."

She scowled at him. "Do you have to eat Jell-O while I'm talking serious?"

"Seriously," he said triumphantly. "It's an adverb."

"I quit work at ten o'clock."

"I'll meet you here then."

"And we'll talk," she said.

"Fine."

"Our discussion will be frank and open."
"And afterwards we'll issue a joint communiqué."
"And we won't make jokes. This is serious."
"Right. Can I have another Jell-O?"

At fifteen to ten Cody showed up and bought a small
bowl of grapes and sat at a booth while he waited for her
to finish work.

A few minutes later she sat down with him. "Want to
know what I did this summer?" he asked.

"Sure."

"I worked for a highway construction company in
Nevada. Here, I'll show you where I was." He started lay-
ing grapes down on the table. "Okay, this grape is the
northeast corner of Nevada, and this grape is the north-
west corner, and this grape is about where Reno is, where
the boundary bends to make the left branch of its V-
shape. Okay? And this grape is the southernmost point
of the state. You got it so far? This grape is Las Vegas.
Okay now, this grape goes where I worked this summer."
He placed it carefully on the table. "It was near Win-
nemucca. We were building twenty miles of new road."

While he enthusiastically explained some of the details of his summer job, she absentmindedly reached
down and picked up a grape from the table and popped
it in her mouth.

"Oh, no!" he moaned. "You just ate Las Vegas."

Giggling together, they then proceeded to eat the entire state of Nevada.

"Where do you want to talk?" he asked later, as they
walked outside.

"Anywhere—it doesn't matter."

"How about in the parking lot outside your dorm?"

"No, not there," she said.

"You said anywhere."

"I meant anywhere but there."

"Why not there?"

"Because that's where we always ended up after a date."

"And that's bad?"

"It's not bad—it's just that this isn't that kind of a date. This is a discussion date."

He shrugged his shoulders. "Where do people go for discussion dates?"

"I don't know. I've never had one either."

"The library?"

"It's closed," she said. "I know—how about the Eyring Science Center by the Foucault pendulum."

He nodded. "Right—this is going to be a pendulum kind of date."

They walked to the science center. The back doors were locked.

"There're always graduate students around a place like this," she said. "Can we walk around and look for lights that are on?"

They started walking. "There's a moon out tonight," he said, reaching for her hand.

She pulled away. "This isn't that kind of a date."

"It's not my fault the moon's out. I had nothing to do with it. Honest, it just came out on its own."

They walked to the front door and peered in. It was locked.

They turned around. They were facing a statue of Dr. Eyring. "Think of all that science has given the world," she said.

"I am," he said, putting his arms around her. She momentarily allowed herself to relax in his arms. He was about to kiss her.

She broke away. "This is supposed to be a discussion date, and you're ruining it."

"It takes two to ruin," he said.

"Cody, we've got to discuss something very important tonight."

"All right, all right. Discuss."

A sleepy graduate student opened the door to leave

the building. Cody grabbed the door before it closed, and they went in. The lobby was dimly lit. She asked him to stand opposite her across the twenty-foot circular framework for the Foucault pendulum.

"Women have come a long way in our time," she said. Her voice echoed in the large, dark room. The red light from the exit sign made them just visible to each other. "In the fields of literature, business, law, and science, women are now making their presence felt."

"Excuse me," he called out, "but should I be taking notes?"

"That's just like a man," she fumed. "You don't treat what I say with the least degree of respect. And you don't respect women. Women are just as capable of doing great things as men. They're just as smart, just as creative, and just as capable. In some cases, they're more capable. It's not right to limit a woman in any way."

"I'm not."

"Society does, and you're part of society. Have you ever heard of a right-hand woman? No. Why not? I'll tell you why, because we live in a male-biased society. That's why." Her voice was rising. "Listen to me. When I chew out that idiot French horn player because he can't carry a tune in a bucket, I'm still feminine. Feminine doesn't always have to be sweet, does it? Of course not! Sometimes feminine is angry! Why can't that idiot play what's written at G?"

He was looking at her strangely. She realized she'd been shouting.

She paused to gain her composure, cleared her throat nervously, and then continued in a lecture style. "Of course, it's true that women have babies, and that in itself makes them unique, but we should never overlook their other attributes."

"I never do," he said, smiling broadly.

She scowled. "You had to say that, didn't you. Well, anyway, take Lisa Salinger as an example."

"Who's Lisa Salinger?"

"She's the one who discovered the Grand Unified Field theory."

"Oh yeah—isn't she the one who sleeps on a roof and eats lawn clippings?"

"It's a storeroom where she sleeps, and it's not lawn clippings she eats. It's wheat and alfalfa sprouts."

"Well, that certainly sheds a new light on things. I have a completely different picture of her now. Oh, I also read she talks to rats, wears sheepskin pajamas, and gargles yogurt."

"She doesn't talk to rats! Well, okay, once she talked to a mouse, but good grief, it was just one mouse. And she doesn't have sheepskin pajamas. She has an old sheepskin coat that occasionally, on very cold winter nights, she wears over her nightgown. And she only gargles yogurt when she has a cold. Mostly her roommate made up those lies."

"What makes you such an authority on her?"

Dawn paused. "I wrote a report about her for a summer class."

"Okay, she's not quite as crazy as people think she is. So what?"

"She's a woman."

"Right—that's what you'd expect from someone named Lisa."

"Lisa Salinger did something that not even Albert Einstein was able to do."

"Okay, fine. She's the next Einstein. So what?"

"I want you to learn to like her."

"Why? I'll never meet her."

She paused, fighting for the right way to let him know who she was. "Let me say this another way. Before our relationship gets too serious, you need to understand something about me."

"And what's that?"

She wiped her damp brow. "It's kind of hard to explain."

"Well, go ahead and try."

Her hand was tugging nervously at a strand of hair. "Maybe if I give you an example. Two trains are approaching each other, each going forty miles an hour. When they start they're two hundred miles apart. There's a bird that can fly one hundred miles an hour. When the two trains begin, the bird starts at train A and flies to train B, then turns around and flies back to train A. He keeps doing this, going back and forth. Question: How far does the bird fly before the trains collide?"

He paused. "Is this important?"

"It's very important."

He shrugged his shoulders. "I don't know how far the bird goes. I can see that the distance he has to travel keeps getting shorter as the trains approach each other."

"That's right."

"I'd need some time to work on it."

"You don't know the answer, but I do. How does that make you feel?"

"It's your problem—I'd expect you to know the answer."

"But what if I gave you ten minutes to work on the problem, and you couldn't work it. How would that make you feel?"

"I could figure it out if I really wanted to."

"Maybe. But what if you couldn't, and what if I told you I can do the problem in my head. How would that make you feel then?"

"Hey, no problem," he said with his hands up for emphasis.

"You wouldn't be threatened by that?"

"No."

"The answer is two hundred and fifty miles. It doesn't threaten you that I can work it in my head?"

"Why should it? Just because you can work a dumb problem about a bird? You think that bothers me? It doesn't matter, really."

"It's very possible that I'm smarter than you are."

"In some things maybe, but I'm smarter than you are

in other areas. When it comes to doing anything outdoors I'm better. I can hike better, fish better, hunt better, and run a survey crew better."

"But what if I'm really good in math? I mean super
good."

"Fine."

"You wouldn't be at all threatened by that?"

"No. Why should I be?"

"You're sure?"

"Of course. I'm very open-minded."

She sighed. "That's good."

"So you know how far the bird flies. Is that your secret?"

"That's not all. Listen to me—I want to tell you something I've never told anyone before at BYU."

"I'm listening."

"You've got to promise not to tell this to anyone."

"I promise."

"Okay." She looked around to make sure nobody else
was listening. "There are four basic forces in the universe: the gravitational force, the electromagnetic force,
the strong nuclear force that binds protons and neutrons
inside the nucleus, and the nuclear weak force. The electromagnetic, strong, and weak forces have all been described by quantum theories, which says that the force is
carried by small packets of energy. For instance, in the
case of light, the force carriers are called photons. For a
long time scientists had hoped that the four different
forces might be manifestations of a single underlying
law. The problem was that the gravitational force refused to fall into line, until Lisa Salinger came up with the
Grand Unified Field Theory."

He paused. "That's cute. Where'd you memorize that
from?"

"Cody, my secret is I'm a genius."

"Hey, no problem. It doesn't change anything."

"Do you mean that?" Her expression suddenly
brightened.

"Sure. So you're a genius. I can handle that."

"All right! Cody, I now declare this discussion date to be over!" She ran into his arms.

A minute later they started toward the door. "It was so hard for me to tell you. I was afraid you'd be intimidated."

He put his arm around her and hugged her. "My little genius," he said.

She scowled and backed away. "You don't really believe me, do you."

"Why do you say that?"

"The term 'my little genius' is demeaning."

"What's demeaning about it?"

"*Little*. It's like 'the little woman.'"

"What do you want—my big genius?"

"I'm not big."

"Okay, how about my genius then."

"That's better—except I'm not yours in the sense of property, as in 'my car.'"

"How about saying, a genius who—I mean whom—I love."

"That's okay."

He breathed a sigh of relief. "Terrific—I got it right. Let's go celebrate. How about buying enough grapes to map out the entire continental United States?"

They walked to his car. "So your big secret is you can do bird and train problems. Is that it?"

She hadn't actually told him she was Lisa Salinger. *I'll save that for later*, she thought. *First let him get used to me being a genius.* "That's right."

"I thought it was something serious."

"Nothing very serious," she said lightly. "Can you come over for supper Sunday?"

"Sure."

"I'll bake some bread for you. I learned how last summer."

A few minutes later they walked up to the dorm.

"Crazy lady, I'm pretty sure I love you. Hey, I've got a bizarre idea. Why don't we get engaged tonight?"

She giggled. "Really? Are you serious?"

"But it's only because you have a cute nose." He kissed her nose.

"Give me a good reason why our getting married would be a good idea," she said, trying to be objective.

"I love you. That's reason number one."

She suddenly moved away. "You love Dawn."

"Right. That's your name, isn't it?"

"I have two names. You know only one."

"Is this another problem, like the one about three missionaries and three cannibals, and they have to row across a river on a boat that will only take two people, but if you ever have two cannibals and one missionary together, the cannibals will eat the missionaries? Okay, I give up. What's your other name?"

"Lisa," she said.

"That's your middle name?"

"Yes."

"That's the same as your weird friend."

"She's no weirder than I am."

"If you say so. Dawn Lisa, will you marry me in the temple in about three months?"

"In the temple?" she asked.

"Sure. Is there any other way?"

She still wasn't a member of the Church yet, though everyone thought she was, thanks to her access to the school's computer files. "There may be one or two things we need to talk about before then."

"You want to talk about them now?" He looked into her eyes, holding both her hands.

She shook her head wearily. "No way. This is plenty for one night."

CHAPTER EIGHT

Cody invited her to spend the next weekend at his parents' home in Ogden. The entire family was getting together. As they drove there Saturday afternoon, enjoying the beauty of the fall, he described his family to her. His older brother, Darin, was married to Gail. They had four children, the oldest being seven years old. He also had a sister two years younger than he. Her name was Dianna. She was married to Kirk and had two children, a girl two years old and a boy six months old. There was also a seventeen-year-old sister, Heidi. She was a junior in high school. Next came fifteen-year-old Alan, and then eleven-year-old Josie.

She met the members of the family all at once, and it took a while to get them all straight in her mind.

The family lived in an older brick home in an established part of town. It was not a large home, considering the size of the family, but it did have a certain charm. In the backyard was a treehouse for the children, as well as a garden that was still producing a large variety of vegetables.

Cody's father was a building contractor. Like his son, he was full of jokes. He loved to play with his grandchildren, and he spent much of Saturday giving rides on the tree swing. Sometimes, with a magician's wave of his hand, he'd find a piece of candy hidden in one of their ears.

Cody's mother had gray-blue eyes and ash-brown hair, flecked with strands of gray. Worry lines had begun to mark her face, but she was still beautiful. She hugged her grandchildren every time they got close enough to her.

To Dawn it seemed like a circus, with kids and dogs and bowls of snacking popcorn together in the small living room.

Cody's father, seeing her experiencing culture shock, came up to her and said quietly, "Come on outside with me. I want to show you something."

They walked through a small kitchen full of good smells and out the back door. On his way out, he picked up a salt shaker.

He showed her his tomato patch. "Pick a couple of tomatoes for us."

"It's a wonderful garden." She carefully pulled off two large tomatoes.

"Smell your hands," he said. "Isn't that wonderful? You get it anytime you work around tomato plants." He gave her the salt shaker. "We'll have to be careful we don't get seeds on our clothes. We wouldn't want to give ourselves away. Spoiling our supper, that's what my wife calls it. I don't know why—eating before supper never hurt my appetite."

She took a bite of tomato. The warm tomato juice seemed to explode in her mouth. She sprinkled some salt in the open part of the tomato.

He took a bite and grinned. "We're rich, you know that? Anytime you can walk out in your garden and eat a whole tomato from the vine, you're rich as Rockefeller."

"It's delicious."

Cody was in the front yard teasing his nieces and nephews. He galloped into the backyard with one on his back and others chasing him.

Noticing that their grandfather was outside, the children came around and begged for a ride on the tree swing. They kept him busy.

Alan, the fifteen-year-old, came out looking for her. "Cody says you like math. Want to see my computer?"

They went to Alan's room. He turned on his computer and the TV monitor. "I bought this with money from my paper route. Last summer I spent about five hours a day programming it. I'm working on a game program. I want to enter it in a contest Atari sponsors and see if I can start getting royalties from it. Want to see it work?"

"Sure."

A few minutes later they went over the program step by step, trying to rewrite it so it'd run faster. "If that's still not fast enough," Dawn said, "I'd suggest you switch to machine language. Initially it'll be a pain to program, but it'll speed things up. I'll send you a book that might help."

"Thanks. Oh, by the way, I'm glad Cody's going to marry you."

"Thank you."

She went into the living room. The men were sitting around talking.

"Dawn, the women are all in the kitchen helping get supper ready," Cody said.

At first she didn't understand what he meant, but then she realized he wanted her to go out there too. She wanted to stay in the living room with the men, who were talking about building ultralight planes from a kit. She was worried that if she went into the kitchen, she might be asked to do something she didn't know how to do. Cooking had never been of much interest to her. All the time she was growing up, feminist leaders were encouraging girls to escape the drudgery of housework and do something significant with their lives. She had gladly followed the advice.

That's why she liked canned soup.

But she could see that Cody wanted her to help out in

the kitchen, so she decided to go see what homemakers do.

"Can I help?" she asked weakly when she entered the kitchen.

"We never turn down offers to help," Cody's mother said. "What would you like to do?"

She paused, not knowing what to say.

"You can take my job," Dianna volunteered. "I've got to go nurse my baby."

"Oh, don't go, Dianna," Cody's mother said. "You can nurse in here. We'll just tell the men and boys to stay out."

Dianna showed Dawn how to make a radish look like a flower, then picked up her baby, put a shawl over her and the baby, and started nursing.

As she worked on the relish tray, Dawn often looked up to watch Dianna. It was the first time in her life she'd ever seen a woman nurse. In fact, she didn't know people did that anymore. She was both curious and a little embarrassed. Dianna, however, seemed quite at ease.

The women were cheerful. They didn't seem to mind doing all the work to prepare the meal. And she had to admit a certain pride in each radish flower she turned out.

Dianna stopped for a minute to burp her baby. A large noise erupted, and she laughed. "That's my boy," she said. He laughed. "Are you my lunch mouth?" she asked. The baby laughed again. A pattern developed. Each time she made a funny face and asked if he was her lunch mouth, he laughed.

The laugh began in his toes and rumbled and tumbled through his body until it rushed out. Dawn felt a tugging at her heart, a yearning to have her own baby.

"Okay, kid, the fun's over," Dianna said. "Lunch time again." She looked up and noticed Dawn watching. She smiled. "I love doing this for my baby."

"Was it hard at first? I'd have no idea how to even start."

"Nature does most of the work. The rest is just patience."

"Dawn, you've been so quiet. Tell us all about yourself," Cody's mother asked.

She told the things she'd invented about Dawn Fields. They seemed willing to accept it, even though, she painfully reminded herself, it was all a lie. She was an imposter in their home.

They trust me, she thought. *But I'm not Dawn Fields, and I'm not a member of the Church, and I can't be married to their son in a temple.*

"Well, I think we're almost ready," Cody's mother said a few minutes later. "Let's dish out the children's plates first. They'll eat on the picnic table outside."

A few minutes later the family knelt in family prayer around the kitchen table. Cody's father offered the prayer. He thanked God that the family was all together again; then he prayed for a blessing on the food.

Suppertime was full of old jokes and good food and kids running in and out of the house, asking for more food or reporting who pulled whose hair or which cousin dumped his beans in the garden.

Afterwards the men volunteered to clean up, and the women sat in the living room and wondered how many plates would get broken before the job was finished.

"Can I hold your baby?" Dawn asked Dianna.

"Sure. Put this shawl over you in case he spits up."

She held the baby in her arms. He was sleepy and warm and cuddly. He gently tugged at her hair. After a few minutes, he fell asleep.

"I can lay him down if you want," Dianna said, picking him up and taking him away.

They decided to have family home evening. It was held in a mammoth tree with huge branches, set on a hillside near the house. The tree was easy to climb by approaching it from the uphill side.

"This is our family tree," Cody's father joked as he

boosted Dawn up on a branch next to Cody. Children and parents were strung all along the lower branches.

"How come we can't be on that branch?" one of the kids complained.

"Because you can't," his cousin said.

"It's not fair. They got the best branch."

The parents tried to stop the bickering.

Cody's father laughed. "Family home evening is the only argument that begins and ends with prayer."

They sang a song. The sound boomed over the valley. Then one of the grandchildren offered a prayer.

"And now the Wells Grandkid Choir will sing some songs for you."

"I don't want to sing," a slacker complained.

Dianna led them in singing "Pioneer Children." The voices came in scattered formation with the younger kids always a little late, one older kid always out of tune, one trying to sing as loud as he could, one hanging back, another just standing there resentful of the whole idea. When it was finished, their grandfather praised them and gave each one a stick of gum.

"We're happy to have you all here tonight," Cody's father began, "especially to have Dawn here with us. We're delighted Cody's found such a lovely girl to be his bride."

"Relieved is closer to the truth," Darin joked.

"Well, anyway," Cody's father continued, "I want all of you to know there's nothing in my life that's given me more joy than my family. I love you all. Dawn, we'd like to hear from you now."

They helped her out of the tree so she could stand and talk to them. "I've enjoyed being here. The food was delicious. Oh, I hope you all liked your radish flowers Dianna and I made. It's been a lot of fun. Seeing Cody's family, I can see why he's such a special person."

"What temple will you two be getting married in?"

Suddenly she felt terrible.

Cody helped her out. "I think probably the Provo Temple, because we see it every time we go on a date. That'll always be our temple."

"Are you all right?" Cody's mother asked Dawn, whose face was flushed.

"It must've been the hike up here to the tree," she said, wiping the perspiration from her face and sitting down on a large rock to rest.

At the request of the grandchildren, the entire family played Hide and Seek until it got too dark. Then they went inside and had ice cream and raspberries from the garden.

Finally it was bedtime. Darin and Gail wandered around the house trying to find scattered shoes or socks or sweaters before they left for their home in Logan. Dianna and Kirk, who lived in California and were out for a visit, bedded down their family.

Dawn was to sleep in seventeen-year-old Heidi's room. Because she was a guest, she was given first chance at the bathroom. When she finished, she returned to the room and looked around. Track medallions and ribbons hung from Heidi's bulletin board, and a certificate naming her the most-improved choir singer in her sophomore year hung on the wall. There were also two pictures of boys. A poster of the Ogden Temple hung over the bed, and a copy of the scriptures lay on a nearby table. Dawn picked up the Bible. Certain passages throughout were marked in red.

On a dresser she saw a beautiful booklet, apparently used by girls in the Church to set their goals in life. A girl was encouraged to set a goal in each of several areas of importance. She wanted to see what goals Heidi had set but decided it would be an invasion of privacy. She put the booklet back.

There was a knock on the door. She opened it, and Cody's mother entered.

"How are you feeling now?"

"A lot better, thank you."

"Here's an extra blanket if you need it."

"Poor Heidi. I feel bad about kicking her out of her bedroom. Where's she sleeping tonight?"

"Oh, don't worry about her. She'll be sleeping in our camper. I think she prefers it there anyway."

"I'll thank her in the morning."

"Fine. Oh, do you have a minute? I want to show you something."

They walked downstairs. In a corner of the basement, Cody's mother turned on a bank of lights. There on an easel was a watercolor painting.

"This is what I do to keep my sanity. Over there is a stack of the ones I've finished."

Dawn went through them one by one, mostly landscapes but also a few portraits.

"I like them very much," Dawn said.

"It's good therapy. Sometimes when I get in the mood, I come down and paint and just forget about all the have-to's in my life. I work down here for a day or two, and then I'm okay and can go back and take care of my responsibilities again."

"You're really happy with your life, aren't you," Dawn said.

"Very much, and you will be too."

"Do you ever wish you had a career?"

"Well, of course, I have worked. I had a job while Cody was on his mission. I was good at it, and sure, there was satisfaction in earning money, but my career is being a wife and mother. It's what I most enjoy doing. I love it when my kids run in the house and yell, 'Mom, guess what happened?' And I enjoy it when my husband comes home from work and tells me how his day has been. I just love what I do. Sure, I know that sometimes mothers have to get jobs out of economic necessity, but I'm glad we've been able to manage most of the time on what my husband earns. All in all, I guess I'm about as fulfilled as I want to be."

Dawn nodded. "I admire you."

"What about you? Will you work after you're married?"

"I don't know yet," Dawn admitted. "I'm having a little trouble sorting out my life."

"It'll come. Don't worry, you'll do just fine. You know, I've prayed for Cody's future wife since he was born. I've prayed that she'd be true to the gospel and worthy to be married in the temple, and now look, here you are."

Dawn turned away, feeling miserable again. "I'd better get some sleep now."

"Of course. Good night."

Dawn went to her room, crawled into bed, and cried quietly so that nobody would hear.

After church and lunch on Sunday, they returned to BYU. As Cody drove, Dawn put her head on his shoulder. She had to tell him that she wasn't Dawn Fields and that she wasn't even a member of the Church.

More than ever, she wanted to be baptized. But when she was baptized, it'd have to be as Lisa Salinger. She wouldn't lie to enter the kingdom of God.

She decided she'd just have to admit to the world her real identity, and then nothing could stop her from being baptized. Of course, it'd put her in the public eye again, but maybe the news media would leave her alone. There hadn't been much interest in Lisa Salinger lately.

She wondered if Cody would accept her as Lisa Salinger. He said he didn't mind if she was good at math. Now all he had to do was accept her as Lisa Salinger. She had it all worked out: She'd tell him who she was, and then she'd be baptized, and then they'd go to the temple and get married.

As they kissed at the door, she decided to tell him the next day.

She entered her room and found that Robyn was still at her parents' place. As she got ready for bed, she daydreamed about Cody. She recalled how that morning at his parents' home she'd been awakened by his gentle knock on her door. Knowing that he was just outside in the hall, she wanted to ask him to come in. It would've seemed natural for him to come in, sit down on her bed, and give her a good-morning kiss.

She decided she was ready for marriage.

She thought it would be nice to have some dreamy music to go to sleep to. Maybe she'd dream about Cody.

She turned on the radio. The news was on. ". . . unique in several ways. First of all, it represents only the third time the Nobel Prize in physics has been given to a woman. Some have suggested that the committee was under considerable pressure to award at least one of the Nobel Prizes this year to a woman. Secondly, this year's winner, Lisa Salinger, has for the past year completely dropped out of sight. It is believed that she is living somewhere in California under an assumed name. The Nobel committee was unable to contact her to let her know of her selection. It isn't clear at this time whether she'll even appear in Sweden in December to accept the award.

"Salinger will be remembered by the publicity she received two years ago when a professor at Princeton with whom she had been working charged that she had stolen his ideas and published them. In subsequent hearings, it was determined that the charges were false.

"Salinger takes on the image of Albert Einstein with this award, since Einstein spent several of his last years trying to come up with the same theory. In addition, although Einstein did not receive the Nobel Prize until he was forty-two, most of the work for which he received the prize was done while he was still in his twenties. Salinger at twenty-four will be the youngest recipient in history, beating William Lawrence Bragg, who in 1915 received the award in physics at age twenty-five for the study of crystal structure by means of X rays.

"In the past the Nobel judges have been extremely conservative, usually waiting at least ten years after significant research is published before considering a scientist for such a high honor. In contrast, Salinger's work was published just two years ago. A spokesman for the Nobel Foundation has indicated that the reason for the lack of delay in Salinger's case is that recent experimental work from several areas of research has verified the predictions made from her Grand Unified Field Theory.

"The awards will be presented December 10 in Stockholm, Sweden. Other winners this year include . . ."

In a daze she walked barefooted in her nightgown down to the storeroom. She sat on a trunk and stared at the darkened shadows of suitcases. It was quiet in the dorm. All the good little girls upstairs were asleep in their beds.

And she was a Nobel Prize Laureate.

CHAPTER NINE

The next day Dawn skipped classes and took a long walk on the foothills near campus.

At noon she phoned her mother at the hardware store.

"Lisa, did you hear the news?" her mother cried out. "You won a Nobel Prize!"

"I know, Mom."

"All last night the phone kept on ringing. Reporters want to know where you are. They want to interview you. What shall I tell 'em?"

"Tell 'em I'm coming home. I'll be there tomorrow night."

She made plane reservations to Minneapolis. She planned to rent a car there and then drive to Fargo.

After supper Cody picked her up and they went to the library. She stared mindlessly at the same page for half an hour, then finally shut the book. "I don't want to study," she said.

"What do you want to do?"

"I want you to hold me."

"Nice idea, but I've got all this homework to do."

"What are you working on?"

"Statics and mechanics."

"How long will you be?"

"I don't know. I've been working on one problem for two hours and still haven't got anywhere."

"Mind if I look at it?"

He shrugged his shoulders. "Be my guest."

She read the problem. A few minutes later she wrote down several equations. "May I use your calculator?"

A short time later she handed him the answer. "Now will you hold me?"

He looked in amazement at her equations. "How did you do this?"

"It's like the train problem. There's a hard way and an easy way. I always try to do things the easy way. Now can we leave?"

"Good grief," he said quietly.

He drove her to the parking lot outside the dorm.

"I've got to go away tomorrow for a few days," she said.

"What for?"

"My aunt's sick. She asked me to come and help out. It shouldn't be very long. Cody, please hold me. I want to be in your arms again."

He put his arms around her. She started crying. "You must really be worried about your aunt," he said.

The next day she flew to Minneapolis, took a cab to a motel, checked in under a fictitious name, changed her identity back to Lisa, took a cab to the airport, put a suitcase with Dawn's clothes in a locker, left twenty dollars in the locker in order to reserve it for more than twenty-four hours, rented a car under Lisa's name, then started for North Dakota.

Lisa Salinger's hair had been short, but in the two years she'd been at BYU as Dawn, she'd let it grow out. The day before she returned to North Dakota, she'd bought a short wig to preserve the Lisa look.

Four hours later she arrived in Fargo. When she approached the apartment her mother lived in, she continued on without stopping because the entire block was filled with cars and TV crews. She took the car to a service station and asked if she could leave it there for a couple of days, then took a cab to the apartment and bravely stepped out.

"There she is!" someone yelled.

She met her mother on the landing. They hugged each other. A crowd of reporters took their picture. Her sister Karen, now six months pregnant, was also there. The three of them hurried upstairs with reporters following close by. Finally they reached her mother's apartment, went inside, and slammed the door shut.

A representative of the media knocked on the door and requested a news conference. Lisa agreed. Arrangements were made for it to be held at her old grade school in an hour. TV crews hurried over to set up.

Lisa went to her room and looked at herself in the mirror. With the glasses, the wig, and the gray dress, she didn't look anything like Dawn. She had to protect Dawn and Cody because all this would destroy what they had together. In a way she was grateful to Kimberly for creating a distorted image of her. Kimberly had created a monster, and all Lisa had to do for the next few days was to be that monster.

At the news conference her grade-school principal took charge, introducing her mother and sister to the media and pointing out that they were in the same school where Lisa had first shown promise in science. Then he turned the time over to Lisa.

She began with a statement to the press, which she read. ". . . I'm pleased to be chosen for this honor. There are many others who paved the way for me to come up with the Grand Unified Field Theory. I would like to thank the faculty of Princeton University for their part in this. Thank you."

Ten hands shot up, and everyone started asking questions at once. The principal, used to unruly classes, stepped in. "Not all at once! Okay, you first."

"What does this award mean to the women's movement?" a reporter asked.

"I believe it shows that women can compete with men in any arena."

A man interrupted. "Some say the only reason you received this is because of political pressure exerted by feminist groups to have more women recognized. As you know, during the week the Nobel committee was meeting, women were outside picketing in the streets. Don't you think this might have affected their decision? Also, why should a woman be given this award on work done only two years ago, when typically everyone else receives the prize for work done ten or twenty years ago?"

Lisa answered. "The experimental verification by Tanaka in Japan and by the CERN group in Europe have been important to the validation of my work. That may explain why the Nobel committee felt justified in giving the award after only two years. As to the first part of your question, I would hope my work was judged on its own merits and with no regard to my being a woman."

"If you were married, would you take a back seat to your husband?"

"How do you mean?"

"Would you ever give up your work as a scientist to be a full-time wife and mother?"

"Let me answer your question using a symmetry argument. Symmetry is an important concept in science. You ask if I could combine my career with marriage, and yet very seldom is the same question asked of a man. That shows a lack of symmetry. Question: Is this lack of symmetry imposed by cultural differences or by nature itself? It seems to many that it has been imposed by tradition. Symmetry considerations alone would lead us to believe it worthwhile for both husband and wife to share more equally the burdens of family and the challenges of professional development." She turned to the man who asked the question. "Let me impose this concept of symmetry and ask you a question: When was the last time you hugged your kids?"

There was an awkward silence.

Another question filled the void. "Is it true you have a sheepskin nightgown, and that you gargle yogurt?"

"Yes, that's all true."

Another reporter: "Is it true that while you were coming up with your theory, you worked in a storeroom and talked to mice?"

"Just one mouse. It wasn't a long conversation."

"Can you tell us where you're living now?" someone else asked.

"I can, but I won't."

"Why not?"

"Because I want to be spared future question-and-answer sessions like this from the media."

She smiled faintly at their laughter.

At the conclusion of the press conference, the women in the audience applauded. Her argument about symmetry was used over and over again. In fact, *Ms Magazine* made her their Woman of the Year.

A few minutes later she left the room, surrounded by reporters. She went home with her mother and her sister. They shut and locked the door, but the reporters stayed in the hall and on the stairs.

At five Karen left to go fix supper for her husband.

At eleven that night several reporters were still waiting outside, hoping for an exclusive interview. Her mother went to bed. Lisa turned on "Nightline."

". . . Salinger seems to have rejected most of the things women traditionally are interested in—marriage, children, nurturing. Frankly, I find that significant."

"Why's that, Dr. Warner?"

"Well, I think it's obvious—she thinks like a man. That's why she's made such progress in her research."

Lisa angrily threw a pillow at the TV.

"We also have in the studio Kimberly Brown. Kimberly, welcome to 'Nightline.' I understand you were Lisa Salinger's roommate at Princeton during the time she was developing her theory. Tell us what she's like."

"Well, she was just a terrifically hard worker. I remember one Christmas when she didn't leave the room for three weeks. We tried to get her to join in caroling with us but she absolutely refused. I guess that's what you need if you're going to get a Nobel Prize."

"You knew her well. Did she show any interest in men while she roomed with you?"

"None at all. In fact, she seems to be generally resentful of men. I tried to line up dates for her, but she always refused."

"Do you have any idea why?"

"Well, as you know, I just finished a biography of her. It's called *Woman of Destiny.* It'll be coming out in a month. When I was doing research for the book, I found out that when Lisa was in junior high, her parents were divorced. Her mother ended up with nothing, and they had to scrape by on very little. That might have caused a lot of the resentment Lisa now feels toward men."

"Some have accused you of exploiting your friendship with Lisa."

"Oh, I don't think of it that way at all. I just want to share some interesting details about a truly great individual."

Lisa felt sick. She went to bed.

She woke up at six in the morning and looked outside. Some media people were still on the lawn. She went back to bed and daydreamed about Cody for another hour until her mother got up.

During the day the apartment was a prison. Her mother went to work at nine. A TV news team hounded her at work, interviewing her boss and the customers who came in the hardware store.

The phone rang all morning with offers. Someone called and asked if Lisa'd like to pose for a men's magazine. She hung up on them and left the phone off the hook for the rest of the day.

Just before noon there was a knock on the door.

"Go away," she said through the closed door.

"Lisa, it's Kimberly and Hal. Please let us in."

She opened the door. Kimberly lingered in the doorway and smiled at the reporters and hyped the book she'd written about Lisa. She smiled for several pictures, then closed the door. "I hate all this publicity, don't you?" Kimberly said with a grin.

Hal put his arm around Lisa. "Well, well—how's our little Nobel Prize winner, hey?"

"Do you mind?" she said, removing his arm from around her.

"Same old Lisa, right? Listen, I hope you're not mad at us for trying to make you a rich woman. Remind me to show you your savings account balance before we leave."

"Mad?" she asked. "Why should I be mad? You've lied and distorted everything about me, so that unless I walk down the street with sprouts hanging from my teeth and rats following me, nobody recognizes me."

"You are mad, aren't you," Kimberly said.

She calmed down. "In a way I guess maybe it's worked out for the best."

Hal patted her on the back. "Good girl. We can work together. Look, there's money to be made. We need to get in now while we can. You're hot now, but in two months you'll be as dead as disco. How many times do you figure you could lecture a month? We'll charge five thousand a shot. Think of it, ten thousand a weekend if we just schedule things right."

"I'm not giving any talks."

"You're tossing away forty thousand a month," Hal said. "Kimberly, tell her about the dress."

"It's coming out next month—the Lisa Salinger designer dress. It has all your equations on it."

"And the sheepskin pajamas," Hal added. "A whole

new line. Oh, the sheep industry asked me to say thanks. Also, they were wondering how you feel about leg of lamb."

"Look, I just want to be left alone."

"I love it," Kimberly said. "I think it works for you. I mean it's so Greta Garbo."

Hal nodded his head. "Go ahead, stay hidden for a few weeks. Just tell us where you are. We won't tell a soul."

"It'll be our little secret," Kimberly said.

"I'm not telling you where I'm living. Now please leave."

"Sure, we'll go," Kimberly said. "But can I use your bathroom for a minute first?"

Kimberly left for the bathroom.

Hal flexed his muscles. "See the improvement? I added an inch to my biceps."

"Terrific," she droned.

Hal showed her how much she'd made in the last six months. A few minutes later, she happened to look back. Kimberly was in her bedroom going through her suitcase. "Get out of there!" she screamed, running to stop her.

Kimberly slammed the suitcase shut.

"Did you find anything?" Hal asked.

"Lipstick, eye shadow, a contact-lens case. Lisa, when did you start using eye shadow, and why don't you have any on now?"

"I want you out of here!"

"I've got it!" Hal said. "She's disguising herself as a normal person."

"I'm calling the police unless you leave!" Lisa shouted.

"We're going. Hey, don't worry, your secret is safe with us," Kimberly promised.

They left.

Lisa hurried to see if there was anything else Kimberly might have found. She went through the suitcase carefully. She couldn't find anything to connect her to Dawn. Dawn's clothes were in a locker in the Minneapolis airport.

Her mother came home at five. "What a day," she said, falling exhaustedly onto the sofa. "I spent the entire time talking to news people. My boss made them each buy something. He had good business. I had a lousy day. You want to know what they asked me? 'How does it feel to be the mother of a Nobel Prize winner?' Try answering that twenty times in a row. 'Why does she hide from the world? Will she ever get married?' I'm tired of questions."

"Sorry, Mom."

"How long are you planning on staying here? I'd like to have some peace and quiet again."

"I'll leave as soon as I can travel without being followed."

"Where are you living?"

"I can't tell you."

"You can't tell your own mother?"

"Mom, if they found out, I'd never have a minute's rest."

"Okay, okay."

They went in the kitchen to fix supper.

"I have a friend," her mother said. "His name is Roy Arnold. He runs an upholstery shop. He's been divorced too. We go to the dog track together sometimes. I wanted you to meet him before you go. He's coming over for supper."

Half an hour later there was a knock on the window. Lisa looked out. There was a man standing on a ladder. She let him in through the window.

"Lisa, this is Mr. Arnold. You two sit down and visit while I cook some hamburgers."

"You can call me Roy. Quite a crowd outside, isn't there? I had the ladder in my truck anyway and figured it'd be a way to get in without having to answer a lot of questions."

"Mom says you have an upholstery business. What kind of upholstery do you do?"

"I do a lot of cars. You get a car about three years old and your upholstery starts to fall apart. Unless you want it to look bad, you need to get new seat covers. Oh sure, you can always get something at K-Mart for next to nothing, but if a person wants quality, he has to pay for it."

"Sure," she said.

"My work's guaranteed too," he said.

Her mother brought in the food. They sat down and started eating.

"Had an interesting thing happen to me today after work," Roy said. "Two Mormon missionaries came by. They go door to door, you know."

"I never let 'em in," her mother said.

"Oh, me either. I told 'em I wasn't interested. Sent 'em on their way in short order."

Her mother nodded her head. "The thing I can't understand is why that religion hasn't died out yet. Sure, they could pull the wool over people's eyes a hundred years ago, but today people are more educated."

Lisa couldn't let that pass. "Mom, you don't know what you're talking about. Brigham Young University is one of the best schools in the country. And there're plenty of scholars and scientists who belong to the Church."

"Maybe so, but they're wrong. I know that," her mother said.

"How do you know if you've never listened to them?"

"Oh, I know. I've heard about their gold bible."

"You mean the Book of Mormon? How can you decide about a book you've never read?"

"Don't need to read it. I know they're wrong. That's all I need to know."

The subject was closed.

Her mother brought in some ice cream.

"Are you going to tell her?" Roy asked.

"Lisa, Roy and I—we've decided to get married. We thought you'd want to know."

"Oh," she said.

"I'll be moving in with him," her mother said.

"But you're welcome to stay anytime you want to drop by," Mr. Arnold said. "We've got an extra bedroom, and if you'll give us a few days' notice so I can get my upholstery supplies out of it, you're welcome anytime."

"Thank you."

They watched TV for an hour before Roy climbed back down the ladder. Just as he touched the ground, a reporter saw him. Roy grabbed the ladder, ran to his truck, and pulled away. As it turned, the lettering on the side of the truck became visible. The reporter stopped and jotted something in his notebook.

Her mother looked out the window and then turned to Lisa. "I'll understand if you can't make it to my wedding."

That night Lisa phoned Cody.

"I miss you," he said. "When are you coming back?"

"Soon," she said.

"How soon?"

"As soon as I can."

"I want to marry you," he said.

"Cody, there's something I need to tell you."

"What is it?"

"I'll tell you when I get back."

Two days later she decided to make a run for it.

She got up at two in the morning and walked through backyards until she got to the gas station where her car was. She drove to the Minneapolis airport, turned in the car, picked up her other suitcase from the locker, took a taxi to a motel, checked in, changed back to Dawn, took another taxi to the airport, and took a plane to Salt Lake City and then a limousine van to Provo.

By the time she got to her apartment, it was eight at
night. She phoned Cody.

"I'm home."

"I'll be right over."

She waited in the lobby for him. As soon as she saw
him coming up the walk, she ran outside and threw her
arms around him.

"I love you," she said.

"Lady, I've been dying to hear you say that again. I
love you too. What is it you want to tell me?"

"Not now."

"I've got a present for you from my mother. It's in the
car. I'll go get it."

He returned with a portrait of Dawn. The face was
full of light and cheer and hope. It was Dawn.

It made her cry to see the painting.

Monday morning when she came out of class, a girl
approached her. "Are you Dawn Fields?"

"Yes."

"The *Universe* wants to do a story about you."

"I don't want a story done about me."

"Just a human-interest feature. You know, where you
went to high school, what you're majoring in, how you
got the idea of starting COEDS, things like that."

"Please, no story."

"I've done some research on you. Do you have a minute?"

They sat in an empty lecture room.

"Your student information form says you're a member of the Church from Grand Island, Nebraska. Well, I
know a guy from there, and he says he's never heard of
you. That's the first question. Are you really from Nebraska?"

"My parents moved there from Fargo, North Dakota,
a few weeks before I left for BYU. That's why nobody
there knows who I am."

"Well, that explains it then," the girl said with a re-assuring smile.

Dawn smiled back.

"But you are a member of the Church, right?"

"Yes, of course."

"So there's a bishop in Fargo who knows you?"

"Yes," she lied.

"Who would that be?"

"They just changed bishops. I don't know who the new one is."

"Who was it when you were in high school?"

"Look, I need to get to class or I'll be late."

"Okay. I'll call you tonight. I thought I'd talk to my cousin too. He's dating a girl from some place in North Dakota. It's either Fargo or Bismarck."

Dawn left. *They're getting closer,* she thought. *How many days do I have before this whole thing blows up in my face?*

Saturday they went for a hike. It was late fall, and there was snow on the top of the mountains. Cody kept telling her how beautiful it all was.

Partway up, they stopped to rest. She sat down on a large boulder. He sat beside her.

"How much farther are we going?" she asked.

"To the top."

She sighed. "Is this my punishment for leaving you last week?"

He laughed.

"Hold me," she said.

"Okay."

"Don't let go."

"They'll find us next spring locked in each other's arms—two giant ice cubes."

"Good," she said contentedly.

"You're ruining my plans," he whispered in her ear.

"What plans?"

"We were supposed to get to the top before I gave you

this." He reached into his pocket and pulled out an engagement ring. He slipped it on her finger. It was too big.

"We'll get it adjusted, but anyway, you get the idea. It would've been much more impressive on top of the mountain, don't you think? Also if we were on top of the mountain, we'd be able to see the temple where we'll be married."

He kissed her.

I'll tell him when he takes me back to the dorm, she thought. But she didn't. He asked her about going to the movie on campus that night. She agreed.

I'll tell him before the movie.

She went back to her room and took a long shower and then did her hair.

Tami came in the bathroom, also in the process of getting ready for a date.

"Can I talk to you?" Dawn asked.

"Sure. What's up?"

"I'm not really a member of the Church."

"You aren't? Why not? You live like you are."

"I want to be. It's a long story. Cody doesn't know yet. I'm going to tell him tonight, and if he's understanding, then I'll get baptized and we'll be able to get married in the temple."

"I guess you know about the required year's waiting period between the time you're baptized and when you can go to the temple."

"A year?"

"Yes. The reason I know is because my brother-in-law had to wait that long before he and my sister went to the temple."

Dawn went in her room and closed the door and cried.

The movie was a comedy.

I'll tell him when he takes me home.

They went to the snack area and had a cherry lime.

Gary Doyle came up to them. "Your roommate said I might find you here." He sat down in the same booth. "I

had an interesting phone call the other day from a reporter for the *Washington Post*. He was calling from
North Dakota. It seems he talked to a man at an upholstery shop . . . let's see . . ." He looked down at his
notebook. "Oh, yes, Roy Arnold. Arnold said he'd had
dinner with Lisa Salinger, the Nobel Prize winner, and
her mom a few days ago, and Salinger had defended the
Mormons and BYU. So the reporter called me to ask if
there was any chance that Lisa Salinger might be hiding
out at BYU. Well, I thought that was really a long shot. I
was about to forget the whole thing when Cindy Dyer
came in complaining that she can never get to talk to you.
And some things you tell her just don't add up. For instance, nobody in the Church in Nebraska or North
Dakota has ever heard of Dawn Fields. And the home address you gave in Nebraska is a Burger King. This morning we phoned Grand Island High School and asked
about you. They have no record of a Dawn Fields ever
being there, and yet your transcript shows you as a student there. Strange, right? Today I went to the Physics
Department and nosed around. I met a graduate student. She said she talked to this girl once, a music education major, who told her, out of the blue, that the
Salinger theory is best understood in, let's see what she
said . . ." He glanced at his notebook again. "Oh, yes,
'best understood in tensor notation.' I showed her a picture of Dawn Fields and she said, 'Yes, that's the girl.' Finally we checked the days you've missed class. Guess
what? They coincide with the days Lisa Salinger was in
North Dakota."
    He stopped.
    Dawn was crying.
    "So guess what we concluded? Dr. Salinger, let me be
the first to welcome you to BYU. And thanks for the
story. It comes out tomorrow in both the *Washington Post*
and the *BYU Daily Universe*." He turned to Cody. "How
does it feel to be dating a Nobel Prize winner?"
    Cody sat there stunned.

"Well, I've taken enough of your time already. Enjoy your cherry lime. Oh, before I go, let me lighten things up by telling you this coed joke I heard the other day."

Then he noticed the tears streaming down Dawn's face. "Well, maybe not now," he said quietly, then left.

"You're Lisa Salinger?" Cody asked.

"Yes."

"You're not even a member of the Church?"

She shook her head. "Listen to me, I can join now. Don't you see, I couldn't be baptized before. Not as Dawn. Cody, please, you've got to let me explain why I did what I did. You don't know what it was like as Lisa Salinger. I had to get away. That's why I came to the Y."

"Who's Dawn Fields?"

She wiped the tears from her face. "I made her up."

He stared at the tabletop in front of him. Finally he looked up. "In other words, you've lied to me from the very beginning, haven't you."

"Yes."

"That's the way I figure it too." He stood up, took one last look at her, and walked away.

CHAPTER TEN

The radio alarm went off precisely at 7:00 A.M. She groaned, then sleepily stumbled to the dresser to turn it off. It was September, ten months since she'd left BYU—ten months since she'd last seen Cody.

Much had happened in that time.

On December 10 she had stood in the Concert Hall in Stockholm, surrounded by other Nobel Prize recipients, the royal family, the Swedish cabinet, and members of the Nobel family, as the King of Sweden presented her the Nobel Prize in physics.

She sat on the edge of the bed and tried to wake up.

She lived in an expensive high-security apartment within walking distance of the Princeton University campus. Nobody could get inside unless they rang up first and got permission from a tenant. Hal and Kimberly had picked the apartment for her. The object was to keep away the line of would-be inventors with ideas for perpetual-motion machines, earnest people with petitions for her to sign, and parents of grade-school children who needed help on their science-fair projects. "You gotta be protected from the general riff-raff now," Hal had explained.

Hal and Kimberly arranged all her speaking tours. Except for public appearances, she was left alone so she'd have time to work. In January, she'd begin as a faculty member in the Physics Department at Princeton.

She yawned. She'd been up late the night before working on a paper she would give next month to the American Association for the Advancement of Science.

The building was designed so noises from other tenants were deadened by sound-absorbing walls. She listened. It was quiet.

A few minutes later in the bathroom, she found herself staring at her reflection in the mirror. It was Lisa all right. Lisa always frowned. Lisa was never satisfied. Lisa had to keep working. Lisa had to stay ahead. Lisa had to be independent, because relationships slowed you down and kept you from reaching your goals.

She looked terrible. It wasn't just because her hair needed shampooing, or because she'd quit wearing makeup. Her face reflected a general disappointment, a feeling that there should be more to life than what she had.

She went to the kitchen, poured a glass of orange juice, sat down at the kitchen table, and reread an old letter from Robyn. ". . . Cody phoned a few days ago. He graduated in April, and now he's working on a road construction crew in New Mexico. He asked if I'd heard from you. He said he guessed he should start looking for someone else. He said he needs someone who doesn't mind living in a hot and dusty trailer, a hundred miles from nowhere."

She downed her juice, then went to the window and looked down. Three floors below a man and woman came running out of the apartment and drove away. She wondered where they were going in such a hurry.

Across the street she saw two young girls in a park playing hopscotch. It seemed an eternity since she'd played hopscotch. If she tried now, she felt she'd snap in two like a dried-out twig.

The mother of the two girls crossed the street, took

each one by the hand, and escorted them back to the apartment building next door.

It must be time for school, she thought. *I wonder what they'll have for lunch. I hope it's not tuna casserole. I always hated that. I hope it's pizza and carrot sticks and chocolate pudding. That was my favorite. Girls, I wish you pizza.*

She lay down on the rumpled bed. In her mind she was nine years old, getting ready for school in North Dakota.

I should get dressed, she thought a while later. *I can't just lie around in my nightgown all day.*

She and Hal had developed a work schedule designed to maximize production from her mind. Think of yourself as a factory, Hal had told her.

She heard a baby crying as it was carried down the hall. She frowned. They said she wouldn't hear sounds from the other tenants.

Her sister, Karen, had a baby girl, and a few weeks ago Lisa had held it for a few minutes at the Minneapolis airport. It felt good to have a baby in her arms, but then her plane was called, and she'd had to go.

She turned on her new computer. It was the latest model with all the features money can buy. She put two diskettes into the computer's disk drive. A few seconds later a calendar appeared on the screen with all her appointments for the month. She noticed she was speaking in California that weekend.

The talks were always the same. She was whisked in, gave her talk, and then she was rushed out again—like a circus elephant doing the same trick over and over again. Sometimes she gave three talks in a week, all in different states.

She shouldn't complain. She had everything she'd ever wanted from life—money in the bank, respect from her colleagues. She was fulfilling her destiny. She was the envy of thousands of women and a role model for young girls.

When she next looked at the clock, an hour had passed. She was still in her nightgown, way behind schedule. She'd make it up by working late at night. Lisa always gets the work done. Always, always, always.

While she was looking for clothes in her drawer, she saw her Nobel Prize medallion. She hung it from her neck.

Recently she'd read a biography of Alfred Nobel, the inventor who set up the trust making Nobel Prizes possible. She picked up the book and read a passage that had been haunting her for days. It was from a letter Nobel had written to his brother's wife. "I am disgusted with myself, without rudder or compass, like a purposeless, fate-stricken wreck, without any bright recollections of the past, . . . without a family, which is the only life we may expect beyond the present one, without friends for healthy development of the heart . . ."

Family . . . friends. Suddenly she was remembering her weekend with Cody's family, and especially her conversations with his mother. The Mormons are so naive, she thought, so out of touch with their archaic traditional viewpoint of a woman's role. To teach that a traditional marriage can fulfill a woman these days. Why do they teach it? Don't they know the statistics? Forty-three million women in the work force, triple the number just prior to World War II. Sixty percent of all women between the ages of eighteen and sixty-four are working. Nine million families in the United States where a woman is the only breadwinner.

She looked in her closet, trying to decide what to wear. In the back of the closet she saw a flash of color. She moved aside some clothes and pulled out the pumpkin-colored dress Natalie had once helped her pick out. She'd given away her other Provo clothes except this one dress. It looked completely out of place among the dreary wardrobe surrounding it.

This was Dawn's dress, she thought. She remembered feeling beautiful in it.

Dawn was beautiful.

But Lisa isn't.

She draped the dress in front of her and looked in the mirror. She frowned. It didn't look right.

What would it feel like to be Dawn again?

From a closet she retrieved the painting Cody's mother had done of Dawn.

Dawn, full of light, positive and faithful.

I want to be Dawn again, she thought, at least for a few minutes.

She took a shower and shampooed her hair. It was quite long now. She hadn't the heart to cut it after all the time it had taken to grow. To cut down on the time to keep it fixed, she often wore her wig.

She spent a long time fussing over her hair and putting on makeup. She took off her glasses and put on Dawn's contact lenses, then slipped on the dress.

She looked in the mirror again. There was Dawn. She smiled the way Dawn smiled. It was warm and friendly.

Good grief, she thought, *I'm cracking up.*

The intercom phone was buzzing. She picked it up.

"Are you ready?" Hal asked impatiently.

"Ready?" she mumbled, looking at the clock. It was eleven-thirty.

"You didn't forget the luncheon with the women's faculty club, did you? You're the guest speaker. Get decent—Kimberly and I'll be right up. Buzz the buzzer."

"I'm tired of giving speeches."

"Push the button. We'll come up and talk about it."

She hung up but didn't touch the security release button. A second later the buzzer sounded again. She placed a towel over it.

She picked up the phone and dialed. A few seconds later, Tami Randall in Provo picked up the phone.

"This is Dawn Fields—I mean Lisa Salinger."

"Hey! It's Dawn! She's on the phone!"

Suddenly there were three girls on the phone, all talking at once.

"Quiet!" Tami shouted. "We'll take turns. Let me go first. Dawn, are you still there? We're all just about to go to class. Hey, guess what? I'm taking Introduction to Physics this semester. It's fun."

She let them talk about the details of their life, then she said, "I need to ask a question. What's the most significant thing you feel about yourself?"

The question was passed to the others. They talked among themselves and then Tami came back on the line. "We all pretty much came up with the same answer."

"What is it?"

"That God is our Father. He loves us and wants the best for us. He wants us to be happy and to develop our talents." There was a pause. "Look, can you call back? Maybe tonight. If we don't go now, we're all going to be late for class."

"Sure, I'll call back later."

"Thanks. Dawn, we love you."

She said good-bye and hung up.

She thought it much too simplistic to picture God as a Heavenly Father. Besides, why can't God be female? Or why not just an Essence of All Truth? Why must he be a Father?

She vaguely remembered a song they sing. Something about how in heaven parents aren't single. Truth is reason, truth eternal, tells me I've a Mother there.

A Mother in heaven, she thought. Suppose there are gender differences in heaven—does that mean there are role differences also? And if there are role differences between men and women in heaven, and if heaven represents an ideal existence, then those role differences in heaven, whatever they are, must lead to the greatest happiness for both sexes, even on earth.

If that's true, is it wise to try and remove all role differences on the earth?

Interesting, she thought. If you picture God as an essence, or if you believe there is no God, then you might view all role differences between men and women on

earth to be bad. You might support any movement
whose purpose is to do away with role differences between men and women, with your goal to make men and
women not only equal but, except for childbearing, also
identical.

On the other hand, if you believe God is a Father and
that there is a Mother in heaven for each of us, then you
might decide that some role differences between men
and women should be maintained on earth.

She found herself deep in thought, standing in front
of an open refrigerator door. She grabbed a carrot and
started munching, then went back to a chair overlooking
the window and sat down.

Lisa Salinger proved to the world that, given any
field, a woman can succeed in it as well as a man. But is
that enough for either a man or a woman? Is business or
professional success enough to give purpose and dimen-
sion to a life?

It wasn't for Alfred Nobel. Professional success isn't
enough. People need love and friendship.

The phone rang. It was Hal. He made an effort to
be calm and reasonable. "Lisa, let us come up. Okay,
you don't want to speak to the women faculty today.
Fine. What I'm really worried about is Sunday. You're
supposed to be speaking in Los Angeles, and they're ex-
pecting you there. This isn't going to last forever, you
know. We've got to get in and make it while we can—"

She interrupted him. "Hal, I just need some time to
myself. Look, I'll give your talk in California, but after
that, you and Kimberly are on your own. I can't support
you both the rest of my life. Get a job, Hal—an honest
job, okay?"

Suddenly desperate, he yelled into the phone, "Wait!
Whatever you do, don't hang up!"

She hung up, then took the receiver off the hook.

She went to a bookshelf and picked up her copy of
The Second Stage by Betty Friedan, a leader of the
women's movement. She talked about how, in the begin-

ning of the women's movement, because of their rage at the inequalities they suffered, women were encouraged to escape the confines of marriage and family life in order to seek success in a career. Now several years later Friedan looked at the results. Lisa turned to a page in the book and read it again. *"The women's movement has come to a dead end. . . . Our failure was our blind spot about the family. . . .*

"For us equality and the personhood of women [should] never [have] meant destruction of the family, repudiation of marriage and parenthood, or implacable sexual war with men."

She put the book down and looked at the clock. Lisa is behind schedule today, and there's work to be done. Putting on costume dresses and lounging around all day is not productive. Lisa expects results.

She frowned, thinking how much a bore Lisa was sometimes.

She realized she'd never met her neighbors. She decided to go visiting. At the apartment next to hers she read the nameplate on the door: A. McPherson. *Who is A. McPherson? Have I ever seen A. in the elevator? Is A an Alice or an Arnold? I hope for Alice,* she thought.

She knocked. There was no answer.

Alice was not home. Alice was working hard somewhere so she could earn enough money to continue to afford her privacy in that apartment.

Dawn went to the apartment on the other side of hers. The nameplate indicated that T. Howard Ellison lived there. She knocked loudly. No answer.

"Anybody there? Howard, how do you get in at night? Why haven't I ever seen you? We're neighbors, and I think we should have a brunch for all the other tenants. Howard?"

No answer.

Howard was at work, perhaps in an office cubicle, alone in front of a screen watching green blips that come and go with the speed of light.

She walked to every apartment on her floor and knocked.

Nobody was home, not on the entire floor. She was the only one.

Then she had a frightening insight into the future.

If you teach that people should be free, emancipated, and self-fulfilled, what will eventually happen?

Emancipation will be interpreted as the breaking of family bonds. Eventually society will reach a condition in which an entire civilization lives as individuals in voluntary solitary confinement. Men and women will pursue careers and shun family responsibilities. Neither sex will have any need for the other, except for brief pairings motivated by a search for pleasure. Couples will live together for only brief spans—a night, a month, perhaps a few years, but eventually they'll break up when one or the other wants more freedom.

The children resulting from these brief couplings will be dropped off in the morning and picked up at night—the same as with laundry.

People will end up living alone, spending their lives in self-centered activities—individuals alone frantically doing aerobic exercises in front of a TV set.

Feeling extremely depressed, she returned to her apartment and closed the door. *I've got to talk to another human being,* she thought.

She glanced again at the painting of Dawn Fields done by Cody's mother. Now there's a woman, she thought to herself. A minute later the phone rang at the Wells home in Utah. "Hello," Heidi answered.

"Heidi, this is Dawn Fields—I mean Lisa Salinger. Is your mother home?"

"Sure, just a minute."

A pause and then, "Lisa, is that really you?"

"I hope this isn't a bad time, but I was just looking at the painting you did of me, and I started thinking about things, and I just wanted to talk, if that's okay with you."

"Sure—you know I love to talk. Can you hold on a minute? We're just in the middle of canning pickles, and I need to give Heidi some directions."

Lisa could faintly hear voices in the background: ". . . one tablespoon salt, one bit of dill, and one piece of garlic . . . Okay, I'm back. Where are you calling from?"

"New Jersey."

"I'm glad you called. I've been thinking about you lately."

"I need to apologize for deceiving you and your family."

"No need for that."

"Sister Wells . . ."

"Good grief, Lisa, call me Margaret."

"Okay. Margaret, when I stayed with you, you seemed satisfied with your life. I don't understand that, because you don't have much time for yourself, and your children take up so much of your day. I know you like to paint, but you can't have much time for that. I must really seem incoherent, but, well, I need to know, are you really happy?"

"Oh my yes. I'm very happy with my life. I feel fulfilled as a woman. Just a minute . . . Heidi, there's more garlic in that sack . . . Okay, I'm back again."

"But don't you ever feel boxed in? I mean you seem to always follow your husband. That to me isn't right. I don't understand how a woman can play second fiddle to a man."

"Lisa, the ideal is this: The husband follows the Savior and His teachings, and the woman honors and sustains her husband. Think about the way Jesus treated the women in his life. Any woman would feel comfortable with a man who treated her that way. A man like that wouldn't be a tyrant. He'd be patient, slow to anger, sensitive to a woman's feelings, compassionate and gentle. He'd want his wife to develop her God-given talents."

Lisa paused and then confided, "I've got a problem

with that. First of all, why can't the wife follow the Savior all by herself without her husband being the middleman?"

"She can. In fact, she should. But in a family somebody has to have the final say, and God's established that as the role of the husband."

"It's not fair."

"If the husband cares about the Savior, it's fair then."

Another interruption. Heidi had run out of dill.

While she waited for Margaret to come back on the line, Lisa thought about something Betty Friedan had written, that what was needed in the women's movement now was a new order, where men and women could both be free to develop their potential. What if the new order is already in place? What if it's the gospel of Jesus Christ?

"I'm back again. Any other questions?"

"I don't think so. Thanks. Oh, I hope your pickles turn out."

"They will. It's hard to ruin dill pickles." She paused. "Lisa, Cody still talks about you."

"Tell him not to swear."

Margaret laughed. "Not that way."

"Well, I wouldn't blame him if he was still mad. The facts are that I lied to him."

"We talked about it," Margaret said. "I think he understands now how it was for you and why you went to BYU in the first place. You want to know what he wonders most about? Your feelings about the Church. He'd like to find someone who has the same religious beliefs he does. Lisa, how do you feel about the Church?"

"Well, after the news about me broke and I left Utah, there was the possibility that BYU would press charges against me for breaking into their computer files. It didn't seem like a good idea to be baptized with that hanging over me. Finally they decided to drop charges. But by then I'd been giving all those talks at women's conferences, and, well, some women are bitter that the

Church opposed ERA, and, I don't know, I just never started going to church again. It just seemed easier to stay away."

"That's not what I'm asking. Do you believe the Savior is speaking to a prophet today?"

There was a long pause, and then, "I don't know."

"Before we hang up, let me tell you how I feel about it. I know it's true, and every day of my life adds to that testimony."

"Thanks for telling me that," she said.

"Sure. There's another thing that's worried Cody, and that's how a famous Nobel Prize physicist could ever be content being married to an engineer whose only goal in life is to spend his life outdoors building highways."

"I guess if we ever got together again, we'd just have to try and work it out."

"Sure, like everybody else has to. Maybe I shouldn't be saying this, but I think he still loves you."

"After all I've done to hurt him?"

"Why don't you ask him yourself?"

"Maybe I will."

A few minutes later they hung up. She sat down in front of the window and looked out.

I used to feel that the Book of Mormon is true. What about now?

A sudden fantasy sprang up in her mind in which Cody baptized her and then they got married in the temple.

No, she thought, stopping the dream. *The decision to get baptized has to be based on whether or not I'm willing to live the teachings of the Church. It can't be based on trying to impress Cody. To join the Church just for Cody would be wrong.*

Besides, if the Church is true, it's true for singles, and not just for families. If the Church strives to help families, it also has a mandate to help singles.

And I'd better face it—I may be single the rest of my life.

What does it boil down to? Did Jesus Christ give revelation to Joseph Smith or didn't he? Is the Book of Mormon a second witness for Jesus Christ or isn't it?

Strangely enough, she knew the answer. She'd known for a long time, ever since she'd prayerfully read the Book of Mormon. But other things had gotten in the way.

It's true.

Then I should get baptized. And in order to prove to myself that I'm doing it for the right reason, I won't tell anyone. I won't tell Cody about it. And I won't tell my roommates at BYU.

She paused. *But they're my friends. They'll want to know. Okay, I'll tell them.*

She looked at the clock. It was three-thirty in the afternoon, Eastern time. Only one-thirty in Provo. Too early to phone.

She walked to the window and looked down. The girls who'd played hopscotch in the morning had returned to their sidewalk across the street.

Five minutes later she was outside wearing jeans, a BYU T-shirt, and tennis shoes. "May I play?" she asked the girls.

They looked at her strangely. "Do you know how?" one of them asked.

She smiled. "Well, it's been a long time, but sure I do."

They were much better at it than she was. After flubbing up two times in a row, she started giggling. Then she left them and walked further into the park.

It was a beautiful Indian summer day. The sun felt warm on her face. She walked across the lawn and found a spot and lay down in the sun and closed her eyes. Memories of girlhood drifted into her mind, of being with grade-school friends at the Fargo city swimming pool—how they'd jump in the water and get wet, then jump out again and lie on the hot concrete, their wet bodies making damp shapes on the sidewalk where they lay. She remembered the way the wet concrete and the chlorine in the pool smelled. Sometimes she'd have money for a candy bar, and she'd lie on the warm sidewalk and take a bite and hand it to her friend. At first they'd be shivering, but gradually the sun dried them off. Sometimes they watched high-school girls and privately wondered if their own matchstick bodies would ever turn them into women.

Mostly they hated boys. Boys pushed girls in the water when they weren't ready, and ran on the wet concrete, which was against the rules, and always made the lifeguard blow the whistle. Boys made terrible sounds that girls would never even think of. But sometimes when they were tired of girl talk, she'd purposely linger by the side of the pool hoping to be pushed in by a certain boy with blond hair and blue eyes.

Well, it happened, she thought. *I grew up and became a woman, and yet I'm still waiting to find out what I'm going to be when I grow up.*

What is it that Tami said? The most important thing she feels about herself is that she's a daughter of God, that He's her Father, and loves her, and wants the best for her.

Okay, I'll try it out. I'm a daughter of God. I existed as a woman even before my birth. I'll exist as a woman after my death. I'm important to God because I'm his daughter, and He wants me to improve and progress while on earth.

I need all of me. There's no part of me I can toss away. I need the Child, ready to play and joke and laugh. I need the Adult, the list maker, the achiever. I need the Mother who loves to cuddle a baby. I need the part of me that knows that God lives. I need the Fighter, the one who goes to battle over coed jokes and unfair demeaning attitudes toward women. And I need the Woman who loves being in Cody's arms.

I need Lisa.

I need Dawn.

Not just one, but both. Together as one—fulfilling my destiny.

A fly was buzzing around her face. She sat up and opened her eyes. *I'll go back and make a list,* she thought.

That's what Lisa always does. A list of things I like about both Lisa and Dawn.

She looked around. Across the way a rotating sprinkler was shooting a spray of water across the lawn. She got up and ran as fast as she could toward it. Suddenly drops of water hit like small bombs of awareness on her arms and forehead. She continued running, shouting and giggling in icy delight as the coldness bombarded her body. She forced herself to stand close to the spray as water showered her. She laughed and giggled and shouted at the top of her voice.

The two girls who'd been playing hopscotch were standing by, silently watching her make a fool of herself.

She tried a cartwheel and ended up falling down on the grass.

The girls looked at each other. She was the silliest adult they'd ever seen.

A minute later she retrieved her adult dignity and started home. She reached the sidewalk. Her tennis shoes squished water with each step.

The girls watched her as she passed them.

"Hello again," she said primly.

Back in her apartment, wearing a robe and drying her hair with a towel, she sat down at her desk, turned on the computer and typed on the screen "The Unification of Lisa Dawn." When she finished the two-page list, she printed out three copies to post around the apartment.

At six-thirty she phoned the bishop of the local ward near Princeton. "My name is Lisa Dawn Salinger, and I'd like to be interviewed for baptism."

An hour later she returned from the bishop's office. She felt good. The peaceful feeling had returned. She hoped it would never leave.

She decided to phone Utah again. Robyn answered. "Hello."

"This is Lisa Dawn. Robyn, guess what? I'm going to be baptized."

Robyn screamed excitedly and ran to get everyone else. A minute later, with everyone talking at once, she was welcomed into the Church.

"You've got to tell Cody about it," Robyn said, after everyone else had left.

"Do you have a number for him?"

"Well, he called about a month ago from his company phone in Albuquerque. He spends most of his time in the boondocks, building a highway, so I don't know how you can reach him. But I'll give you the number in Albuquerque. He really sounded lonely when he called me. He's in this dinky little trailer off the side of a highway they're building. He kept talking about how dusty it is, and how he's not sure he could ever ask any woman to live there."

A minute later she phoned the number in Albuquerque and asked to speak to Cody Wells. They said it was impossible. She assured them it wasn't. They said he was a hundred miles away in an area with no phones. She asked how they'd get hold of him if there was an emergency. There was a long pause, then the company president came on the line. He said that if there was an emergency, they'd patch the phone call through onto short wave radio. She asked them to do that.

"Are you sure this is an emergency?"

"It is for me."

"We'll work on it. Give me your number, and we'll call when we're ready."

She sat down and waited.

A few minutes later the phone rang. She picked it up. It was Hal. "We need you to do the TV ad for the Lisa doll next week. It could really be a big number for Christmas."

"Hal, not now. I'll see you and Kimberly this weekend when we go to California, but until then, quit bothering me. 'Bye."

The phone rang again.

"Will you quit bugging me about that stupid doll!" she snapped.

After an awkward pause, the company president said, "I've got Cody on the line, but you'll have to speak loud."

"Cody, is that you?" she shouted. "This is Dawn!"

"Dawn! It's great to hear your voice. I'd better warn you that the whole crew is standing around listening to us."

"I'll remember. Cody, guess what? I'm getting baptized tomorrow."

"That's terrific!"

"I thought you'd want to know. I've had a great day today. I ran through the sprinkler, and played hopscotch with two grade-school girls, and missed an appointment to speak to faculty wives, and talked to a bishop about being baptized, and now I'm talking to you. Oh, I also talked to your mother. She suggested I talk to you. First of all, I want to apologize for misleading you about who I was."

"I've been doing a lot of reading about you. I think I know Lisa almost as well as I knew Dawn."

"Call me Lisa Dawn now, okay? I'm the best of both. Hey, can I come and see you next week? I'll be in California over the weekend, so it wouldn't be that much out of my way. Is it too pushy of me to ask?"

"Not at all! I'd really like to see you again. There's a motel about twenty miles down the road where you can stay. During the day you can come with me, and I'll show you how to build highways." He paused. "Lisa Dawn, I'd better warn you though, things are really primitive here. I mean, the dust is everywhere."

"Hey, I love dust!"

"No kidding?"

"Absolutely! And I like little trailers off the side of highway construction projects—especially trailers that get hot as an oven on a summer day."

Somebody began loudly and ineptly singing the wedding march.

Cody laughed. "Did you hear that?"

"Yeah, I heard."

"What did you think about it?" he asked.

"It was really bad singing."

"It was the wedding march," Cody said.

"I know."

"What do you think about it?" he asked.

"It's a nice song."

He laughed. "You know what I mean."

"I'd like to consider it as a possible option. How about you?"

"Me too. I'd also like to consider it as an option." Suddenly he burst into laughter. "I can't believe this conversation. It sounds like we're about to buy mutual funds. Oh, one other thing about this place—the TV reception is lousy."

"So if we were married, there wouldn't be very much to do at night?" she asked.

"Right."

"We'd keep busy," she said.

"Woooo—eeeeee!" someone on the crew yelled.

"C'mon, guys," Cody pleaded good-naturedly, "Lisa Dawn, we have an electrical generator, so you could use your computer. If we were married, you'd still have a lot of time during the day to work."

"But not at night!" someone teased.

"C'mon guys, give us a break."

The president of the company, listening in Albuquerque, broke in. "And that's an order!" he barked.

A few seconds later it was strangely quiet.

"Lisa Dawn? They all left. Look, if you ever needed to go away for a science meeting, I'd understand."

"I'm sorry for lying to you before. Except for creating Dawn Fields, I'm a very honest person. I won't ever lie to you again."

"I wanted to phone you for such a long time, but I figured you wouldn't be interested in me, not after receiving a Nobel Prize."

"It's nice, but it's not the most important thing in life."

"During the winter, I'll be working in the office at Albuquerque. There's a university there if you wanted to teach or do research."

"Look, don't worry about me. I can do my work almost anywhere. Cody, I'd try and be a good wife and mother. I'd read books about it and talk to your mother. I like her very much."

"Are we really talking marriage as a possible option?"

"I think we are," she said. "But look, don't hang up and panic and think you've just signed your life away. Nothing's official. When we get together, we'll just see how things go."

"You sure you could stand living here? You're not going to believe the trailer."

"Don't worry—I'll make drapes."

He laughed. "You'd make drapes?"

"How hard can it be? I'll read a drape book. Besides, the trailer doesn't matter. Just to be with you, even with both of us covered with layers of dust, would still be heaven as far as I'm concerned."

"Wooo—eeee!" the company president cheered.